MAYA

MAYA

D.N. STUEFLOTEN

FICTION
COLLECTIVE
TWO

BOULDER • NORMAL

First edition
First printing 1992

Published by Fiction Collective Two with support given by Illinois State
University, the English Department Publications Center of the University
of Colorado at Boulder, the Illinois Arts Council, and the National
Endowment for the Arts

Address all inquiries to: Fiction Collective Two, % English Department,
Publications Center, University of Colorado, Boulder, CO 80309-0494

Maya
D.N. Stuefloten

ISBN: Cloth, 0-932511-58-9
ISBN: Paper, 0-932511-59-7

Produced and printed in the United States of America
Distributed by the Talman Company

CONTENTS

PART ONE

PART TWO

PART THREE

PART FOUR

Mä´ya, n. A member of a race of Indians who formerly lived in southeastern Mexico and Central America and are still found in Yucatan.

Mä´ya, n. In Hindu philosophy, illusion, often personified as a woman.

—*Webster's New Twentieth Century Dictionary of the English Language, Unabridged*

PART ONE

1

The white plumeria are at the window, as expected. The woman withdraws her head. The man is in the bathroom to our left. He is shaving. He becomes visible to us only as the camera draws back and turns, slightly. The razor scrapes at his cheek. This scraping is the only sound audible, other than the slight hiss—it sounds like a hiss—made by the film moving through the camera. The camera continues to retreat. It drops lower and *pulls away*. A wide angle lens is used. Our perspective, as viewers, is thus altered in a predictable way. The man recedes to our left, *diminishing* to our left, the woman somewhat less so to our right. *Without moving they draw further apart*. That is the effect we are after. She is lit through the window. The massed plumerias glow in this light. Her shadow crosses to our left, as black as pitch, as black as night, as black—

Only at the very end, with the camera almost on the floor, is the third person visible. It is the priest. He sits at our left foreground, his swollen leg propped up before him. As the scene ends he claps, politely.

2

Her face is at the window. She withdraws her head. *It is the same movement which began the previous scene.* Each scene is thus *a palimpsest.* This cannot be emphasized too much. The white plumeria glow in this light. The camera moves past them, out the window. The outer world is visible below. It consists of green jungle. There are low hills on all sides. Within view is a large, cross-shaped building. This appears to be a church. One side rises into twin towers, or steeples. We are some distance above the ground, perhaps at the second floor of a hotel. The camera drops. Its movements must be fluid. It descends through trees. It descends through giant ceibas, or the yax-cheel-cab, known as the first tree of the world. It descends through red zapotes. It descends through red bullet trees. Other trees will be examined later. Closer to the ground, as we move forward, are the black laurel and the white *Callisi repens.* The camera *fluidly* continues past the ix-batun, the chimchin-chay—it can be boiled, then eaten like cabbages—and the jicama cimarrona, which is eaten only in times of famine. Everywhere are the white plumerias. All throw their shadows directly at the camera: we are moving *into* the shadows, *into* the light. Each species mentioned must be seen briefly: the balche tree, whose bark is fermented with honey; maguey and calabash and chulul trees; the yaxum tree; the num; the chacah, or palo mulato; the white guaje; the chaya, whose leaves are edible. Hanging from the leaves of the chaya tree are pupae, spun by larvae, which will burst, in their season, into blue-veined moths. Visible also—although they remain at the edges of the screen— are the insects and animals. These include the Quetzal bird, or yax-um, in the limbs of the ceiba; the monkey known as maax; the sun-eyed fire macaw; the balam, or jaguar, whose eyes are glowing ochre in this light; the hanging bats which suck honey from flowers; the mut-bird; the long-toed grouse; the opossum; the kinkajou; the fox; the slow moving turtle; the ppuppulni-huh, or swollen iguana, whose eyes are hooded, exophthalmic; two snakes, the nahuyaca, which has four nostrils, and the tepolcua, which will embed itself in a man's anus; and finally the insects: the xulab, or stinging ant; the chac uayah-cab, the stinging ant who lives underground; the cicada and locust; the scorpions, their stingers erect like the organs of importunate lovers; and the false scorpions and the whip scorpions who scurry quickly, from right to left.

The camera moves to the northern doorway of the cross-shaped building just as the man and the woman duck their heads beneath the lintel. They enter from the north. She leads; he follows. Later this order will become important. Within the room—he comes erect as the others enter—is the priest, standing at a display case.

Movement stops for a full beat as the scene ends.

3

The film hisses through the camera. The camera hisses through the room, past terracotta figures, jade masks, carved limestone. The shadows are thrown forward. Her shadow is thrown forward, across us. One can almost feel it: a coolness passing visibly on the screen.

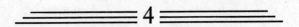

His belly slaps against hers. Her shadow is thrown forward. The film hisses.

5

Because of the shadows it takes a moment for the viewer to recognize what is happening. *This disorientation is deliberate.* His belly slaps against hers. When her face turns towards us we can see the bruise at her eye. A breast is momentarily visible as she turns. The moon is called pach caae. It is the source of light and thus, paradoxically, the source of the shadows. The plumerias at the window are waxy, succulent. Their leaves are pinnately veined. It is known that the sap of these flowers is poisonous. The flowers are visible beyond the visibly slapping bellies.

The woman walks along a path. She wears a white dress. She wears red shoes with high heels. *The camera follows on a parallel at some distance.* She is glimpsed through apertures in the foliage of the yax-cheel-cab, the white guaje, etc. She is seen at the same time as, in the foreground, the kinkajou, the opossum, the slow moving turtle, etc. The ppuppulni-huh rises on its forelegs. Immediately the camera lifts into the air. It rises as the woman hesitates at a red-painted door. Soon we see the cross-shaped building in its entirety. We have risen high above it. The walls of the northern arm of this cross-shaped building are white-painted adobe. The eastern walls are red brick. There is a red ceiba tree next to this eastern wall. The western walls are black, and there are rows of black-speckled corn beyond them. Lintels are of stone, many of them carved. The massive façade of the south is yellow stone. Two towers rise from this façade. In the courtyard below are yellow ceiba trees and yellow bullet trees. The center of the building is a dome made from red brick. It is circular, of course, set into the rectangular belly of the building. The woman is at the western end of the building. She is tiny. She is scarcely visible. Then she is gone.

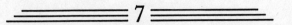 7

The hissing camera moves through the darkened room.

8

They have gone to the doorway. The light is behind them. We are behind them. *They stare forward as their shadows are thrown forward*, away from us, to the edge of the cenote.

The cenote is in the center of the building. It is beneath the dome. Its edges are rugose, but roughly circular. The only light comes from the doorway, *cast forward*, to the edge of this cenote. The husband stands there. He is broad and flat, except for his belly, which falls over the belt of his pants. He seems to have no fear of the darkness. The shadows of the woman and the priest end at his feet. The light comes from the electric bulbs, whose filaments glow like the ochre eyes of the balam. The woman's hair glows, as yellow as the yellow can-lol. She may be perceived as a simulacrum, illuminated, effulgent. The priest is a gnarled figure to her left. Only once does he look toward us, and his eyes are stricken. The woman's lips are glossy, as though waxed. Beyond her the husband is a distant tiny figure, as tiny as a homunculus. His shadow, if he has one, falls into the cenote. Outside—this may be seen, or perhaps inferred—rain has begun. The plumerias open wider. The earth swells like a sponge. The eyes of the balam, or jaguar, glow. They are ochre, like the ochre filaments of the electric light bulbs. "Each bruise is an orgasm." "A virgin death." "Yes, priest, a virgin death." These lines are not spoken. More shadows—that is, the shadow of the priest, who is diminished, and the shadow of the woman, who is enlarged—end at the feet of the husband, whose own shadow, if it exists at all, is cast, and lost, into the cenote.

9

The husband stands at the edge of the cenote. It may be that he has no fear of the darkness. He is broad and flat, except for his belly, which protrudes over the belt of his pants. His hands are thrust into his pockets. He is facing the light that emerges from the room with the red door. The light comes from electric bulbs, whose filaments glow like the ochre eyes of the balam. This light does not reach into the depths of the cenote, which, though irregular, is shaped like a circle. The ceiling is a dome and is set—as we have stated—into the belly of the building. The building itself is shaped like a fat cross. The earth outside—we may infer this—swells in the way a dried sponge will swell when dipped into sea water. Steam rises from the earth. This steam is composed of fetid humors. This rich effluvium is visible. It is as pungent as the farts of old men, as acrid as the scut of the balam. The red plumerias, the scarlet plumerias, the white-petalled plumerias exude odors as dense as oil. The air itself is dense as oil. A swollen iguana moves slowly through this air. A scorpion raises its stinger, from which emerges a drop of poison. This drop of poison is milky white, like the semen of a lover. Hanging from the leaves of the chaya trees are pupae, spun by larvae, which will burst, in their season, into blue-veined moths. Through all of this treads the balam, fur shining with oil, past the ppuppulni-huh, past the erect scorpion, past the maax and the kinkajou, past the opossum and the slow moving turtle, the xulab and the sun-eyed fire macaw. The balam's movements are themselves slow through this turgid air, air dense as oil. In the darkness he casts no shadow.

The woman and the priest cast shadows. Their shadows end at the edge of the cenote, and thus at the feet of the homunculus we call the husband. His hands are thrust into his pockets. He seems to have no fear of darkness. He stares towards the light. "A perfect virgin." "A perfect death." "Yes, priest, a perfect death." The film hisses, audibly, as it speeds through the camera.

"What are you staring at?"

The film hisses—audibly—as it speeds through the camera.

"What are you staring at?"

The film hisses—audibly—

"What are you staring at?"

"Nothing."

PART TWO

1

One lizard eye stares up at her. She lies on a sack bed—burlap stretched over a wooden frame—in a dark corner of the room. There seems to be a lizard at her breast—specifically, a swollen iguana, or ppuppulni-huh, its chitinous teeth fastened at her teat. One exophthalmic eye, with its translucent lid, stares up at her face. Her face sweats, and sweats. Her lips are swollen, bruised. A gecko runs up the wall beyond her. Elsewhere in the room the priest—the man who plays the priest—sits with his face in his hands. The "husband" sits in another corner, a cigarette glowing between his lips. A twist of blond hair lies lankly on his forehead. There is an oily sheen to his face. All of them—all three of the people in the room—are illuminated by the ochre glow of the napalm that flows softly over the hills outside. This glow pulses as each canister of gelatinous petroleum splits open and ignites, one after another. An F-4 Phantom—the smiling pilot is visible through the plexiglass cockpit—banks away from the line of horsemen descending the defoliated hillside. We marvel at the beauty of the scene: the sky to the east a deep purple, the sun rising through the smoke that rises from the ruins of Saigon. Or is it Quang Tri? Or Hue, that ancient city? In any case the horizon is swirling with a smoky, purple glow. Another plane banks away. The pilot, goggled and masked behind his plexiglass, makes a gesture: thumbs up. We watch the line of horsemen descend the blackened slope, threading their way, wearily, between the ochre blossoms of napalm.

The woman pushes the swollen iguana from her breast.

"Are we going to breakfast?"

"We're going to the museum."
"I could use some tea."
"The tea here is terrible."
"So is the coffee."
"At least it's drinkable."
"Just a cup—first—"
"First?"
"Before the museum."
"What difference does it make?"
"I'd like just a cup—"
"The coffee is bad enough, but at least it's drinkable."
"Coffee, then."
"We'll go to the museum first. If you need to drink—"
"Then afterwards—"
"We'll see."
The swollen iguana crawls back to her breast.

Along the tiled floor of the building scutter scorpions. Occasionally the man who plays the husband takes off a shoe and slaps at one. He swears using short, guttural words. Perhaps he is German, or Dutch. We cant be certain. There is no discernible accent when he speaks his lines in English. A good actor, of course, is a good mime. He may be a German actor mimicking American speech patterns, or, equally, an American mimicking a German's profanity. He is blond enough to be a northern European—or an American of northern European descent. His lips are thin, but fleshy. That is, they are not thick lips, but they protrude from his face. They are red and slick, as though perpetually wet. This may be more a characteristic of Germans than Americans. He wears a white T-shirt, as many Americans do. His belly seems soft. It falls over the belt of his pants. His shoes are supple brown leather, moccasin-type. He smokes Gauloises—the pack is in the rolled-up sleeve of his T-shirt—but this may be an affectation. The Gauloises are not necessarily an indication of his nationality.

The scorpions enter the room from the cenote, along with other animals and insects which will be named. The actor lights another Gauloise and blows the smoke toward the woman.

"Let's run through it again."

"No, it's too hot."

"I want it to be perfect."

"I cant concentrate—"

"Just start. Are we going—"

"Are we going—to breakfast?"

"We're going to the museum."

"I could use some tea."

"The tea here is terrible."

"So is the coffee. God, I could use some iced coffee."

"You have no discipline, do you?"

"It's so hot—"

He roughly stubs out his Gauloise. He turns to the window as napalm bursts nearby. For a moment his eyes glow orange.

"Discipline. That's what you lack—what all of you lack."

"All of us?"

"You are too soft."

"It's this heat—"

"The heat has nothing to do with it."

There is a scorpion on the sill. The actor takes off one shoe. He fondles it. He runs his fingers into the shoe, where his toes would go. Then he turns the shoe around and slaps the heel onto the scorpion. He scrapes the carcass off the sill and pushes it along the floor to the foot of his bed. He pushes it into a pile of other dead scorpions.

"The heat," he says, "has nothing to do with it."

He unrolls his pack of Gauloises from his sleeve. He shakes one into his hand. After a moment he puts it between his thin, wet lips. He doesnt light it, however. He continues to sit there. Finally he leans back against the wall, and shuts his eyes.

=========== 3 ===========

A single eye glares at her. He has, of course—the man who plays her husband—two eyes. But it is his affectation to lower the lid of his right eye while staring at the woman. We believe this is a conscious act. He must be aware of the unsettling effect this stare has on her, and on others. His left eye is stern, even mad. It seems paler, a paler blue, than his right eye. Is that possible? The woman turns away from this stare. The iguana, the ppuppulni-huh, crouches on her belly, which is otherwise bare. His tail switches once, twice between her legs. With each switch she gasps, and her face turns further away. Her face is so oily with sweat we are not sorry to have it thus averted. When she speaks, her words are muffled. The husband has to lean forward to hear her.

"I heard screams last night," she says.

"Screams?"

"I'm certain of it."

"I heard nothing."

"I was awakened—they awakened me—"

"Awakened?"

"I dont know the time."

"You were possibly dreaming."

The priest, until now silent in his corner, lifts his head.

"I heard them too," he says.

"You?"

"Distinctly. Quite—quite distinctly—"

"Sound effects."

"What?" says the woman.

"Sound effects," repeats the husband. "If you heard anything at all."

The sun glows through the window to his left. There is a softness to the air that occurs only in the tropics. In this light—especially when augmented by the bursts of napalm—the man seems recognizable. That is, we imagine we have seen him before, perhaps similarly illuminated. He bears a certain resemblance to the film noir actors of another time—Dan Duryea, perhaps, or even Alan Ladd. But their time has gone. If this man is an actor like them, he is an anachronism. It may be he actually appeared in films during the dying days of film noir, or perhaps in the later European films influenced by film noir. If so he must be older than he looks—at least fifty. He would be out of place in modern American comedies about adolescent boys or horror movies filled with plasticized faces and rubbery monsters. Nor would there be a place for him, or for his rapacious glare, in the cineplex boxes which have replaced the grand movie palaces across the American landscape. Perhaps he is aware of this. His soft belly and sallow skin suggest the dissolution of dreams. His thin, wet lips curve into a sardonic grin. Even his presence here, in what must be the lowest of low-budget movie making, is an admission of dispossession. He is dispossessed. He grins, sour, sardonic, sallow, at the sweat-stained body of the woman who plays his wife.

She seems familiar also. We have seen a poster which may be a portrait of her. It achieved some fame during the American-Vietnam War. If it is her, she was both younger and happier then: the skin of her face, in the poster, is tauter, the eyes livelier. Her arms are raised above her head in an attitude of triumph. From her waist to her ankles she is sheathed in white latex pants. Clearly outlined at her crotch are the swelling shapes of her labia major. Because the pelvis is thrust forward, these labia are not only clearly defined by the thin, tight latex, but seemingly *offered*—thrust forward, presented, exposed, delivered to the hungry men of the 9th Marine Expeditionary Brigade and the 173rd Airborne and the 1st Air Cavalry who, at that time, slid through the jungled valleys and denuded back alleys of Vietnam, M-16s cocked, M-60s shouldered, grenades hanging, pockets stuffed with K-bars, C-rations, infrared night sights, packets of C-4, phosphorus bombs and 9mm pistols. How many of these teen-aged lips—most of the American soldiers seemed to be teen-agers—how many pressed hungrily against those printed, proffered labia limned there in those white latex pants? Men jerked off in ditches and foxholes, behind crates of ammunition and in flapping tents. Semen flew through the air like shrapnel, precious seed spilled like blood, bodily fluids exulted, whooshed, blasted like rockets into the thick Vietnamese air. During her tour of Vietnam—it was her apogee as a starlet—she wore the white pants at every stop. She wore them at Da Nang, she wore them at Cam Ranh Bay, she wore them—or a pair exactly like them—at Bien Hoa and An Khe and Phu Bai, even at Bong Son and Nha Trang and, one famous night, at Phuoc Binh. At Phuoc Binh, cheered on by GIs still glassy-eyed from a mortar attack and a fire fight, she—according to rumor—took off the white latex pants: *peeled* them off, peeled them down her hips, peeled them down her thighs, peeled them down her calves, removing and re-tieing her high-heeled, black patent, ankle-strapped shoes, and danced—perhaps for an hour, perhaps *all night*—on a raised platform in front of these desperately hungry men, some still bloody, heads and arms wrapped in mud-stained gauze, uniforms stained, faces stained, bodies thickened and stained with lust, blood, sweat and tears. Is this true? Which battalion, which company, which platoon witnessed this event, which became famous throughout Vietnam? The story, the rumor—true or not—preceded and followed her everywhere she went in that dark, blasted country, like a miraculous vision: labia glossy, engorged with blood, red and slick and swollen—the night brazen, unleashed, still smelling of cordite and death, swollen with the odors of crushed flowers and rotting fruit, swollen with her perfume soured with their sweat, swollen with musky semen, swollen with her dark, effulgent secretions, her black shoes brilliant, beating on tables, beating on counters, beating on platforms, beating on backs, beating in the air, beating while raised high above her head while her white legs flashed in the black, swollen, thick night, the black night which gave way to a thin red dawn, to thin roosters crowing, thin children crying, thin faces emerging, sallow, yellow, exhausted, from bamboo huts, from tin shacks, from holes in blasted walls, from craters in the blasted ground, the ground turned red by the thin, silent sun, and black by the thick, silent, drying blood which stained the earth from border to border to border.

4

The building is shaped like a fat cross. It has been, we are given to understand, constructed—at some expense—as a duplicate of the original building, which is somewhere on the Yucatan Peninsula of Mexico. There is a cenote there, which is a kind of natural well, formed when the peninsula's limestone shelf—a limestone shelf covered by mere inches of soil, a scant country, earth pungent but flimsy, as easy to rip apart as tissue paper—formed, we say, when this limestone shelf is undermined by an underground stream. This limestone then collapses, exposing the water underneath. At the site with which we are concerned, and at many others in Yucatan, the cenote is considered sacred. The most famous example of this, at least to foreigners, is the cenote at Chichen Itza. In some cases—in our case—a temple was built around the cenote. When Francisco de Montejo swept through Yucatan in the service of the Spanish king, this Mayan temple, like many others, was torn down. The limestone blocks, plus additional stones and adobe, were then used to construct a Catholic church on the same spot. This was not seen by de Montejo and the other Spaniards as a desecration, but as proof of the power and rightness of their religion. During the Mexican Revolution, and particularly during the regime of Plutarco Elias Calles, Catholics were persecuted and many of their churches—including the one of which we speak—were closed. It was not confiscated, but neither was it allowed to reopen. Over the years artifacts were brought to it, including some which had adorned the original temple. It thus became, by default, a kind of museum, and remained one until well into the present century, though largely ignored: it was too far from Merida for convenient day trips, and not close enough to any major sites to attract tourists. A hotel was built in the 1930s in a nearby village, but it drew few guests and by the time of our story was largely inhabited, on the upper floors, by relatives of the original owner—primos and tíos, hijos and hijas, abuelitos and cuñados—and on the lower floor by chickens and goats. This hotel has not been reconstructed for this film.

It was a long journey for the three actors to reach this site. They met for the first time in the Hotel Don Jesús. They flew in separately. The woman was disoriented. She staggered down the hotel corridor. "Where am I? Where am I?" Her room was anonymous. It told her nothing. Her luggage was piled all around her. Outside, buses without mufflers snarled past like angry beetles. Everything was hot. Even her air-conditioned room seemed hot. The airplanes, however, had been cool. The airplanes, like the hotel room, had been anonymous. She got on the first one in Iowa. The ticket specified dates and times but said nothing about weather. In Iowa it was always cold, except for the summers, which sweltered. In the airplane the air was thin and chilled. She flew for hours, for perhaps thousands of miles. Clouds passed beneath her at incredible speeds. Yet she sat still. She exerted no energy. When she changed planes she felt expelled—expelled down one chute, into another chute, jostled by strangers who tugged at her purse, who plucked at the sleeves of her mohair coat, whose hands—fleetingly, anonymously—brushed her hips, her fanny, and even her breasts. The caresses were casual, and vanished as soon as she experienced them. Soon she entered another plastic compartment. The seat was comfortable. There was a strange rumble, a kind of pressure, and then silence. People murmured softly around her, as though they were in church. Finally a child began to cry. It cried, perhaps for hours, for thousands of miles, across frontiers, across continents, past ruined civilizations, past third world countries and second world countries and first world countries in the throes of insurgencies and bankruptcies. On the earth far below muggers mugged, judges judged, coups couped, cars lurched off assembly lines, and giant machines stamped out millions of plastic cups. Yet within the plane was audible only a slight hiss, perhaps a faulty air-conditioning vent, and the lonely cry of a single child.

At the hotel she asked the blond man where he was from. He grunted something incomprehensible in reply. It did not sound like the name of a place. They were in the room of the man who looked like a priest. He had instructions, vouchers, tickets spread over a table, but he seemed confused by the whole display. The blond man pouted, and kept muttering his incomprehensible words. A map was spread on the table also, but nothing on it was recognizable.

"Wow," she said. "Did you see those men? At the airport?"

They turned their faces towards her.

"In the blue uniforms. They were cute. You know, sexy. But they had these funny guns—all black, like pistols, but big—"

"MAC-10s."

"What?"

"MAC-10s." It was the blond man, whose single eye now transfixed her. "Machine pistols, my dear. A slight pressure on the trigger—and you are cut in half. Verstehen sie? But you are right. Very sexy."

"Ugh," she said—to herself; the two men had turned back to the map. "No one told me they were real."

5

She enters the train station from the south, preceded by the man.
This order is exactly the opposite of what will occur later, at the
cross-shaped building. It is thus a *mirror symmetry*. All symmetries are
disturbing, but most disturbing of all are the mirror symmetries.
Catching a glimpse of a symmetry in the course of our daily lives is like
seeing the bare bones of a man passing us in the street. Bones are
supposed to be hidden by flesh, flesh hidden by clothes. Bones are
exposed only at times of trauma and death. To see them at other
times—to see a man's pelvis swinging with his walk, a woman's white
scapula poking out of a silk blouse—is to be made aware of our skeletal
understructure, of what supports and moves us beneath our surfaces.
The same is true of symmetries. When a symmetry is exposed we are
seeing something not vouchsafed to most people. Such a symmetry
rouses unease, and when it is a mirror symmetry one may rightly pause,
and gather one's defenses. The woman and the two men are unaware
of this. They take two taxis from their hotel. The woman enters the taxi
from the north, an irrelevancy. One leg lingers for a moment on the
street. It is shapely in a high-heeled pump. The foot is planted firmly
on the pavement, thus exaggerating the arch of her instep. Motor-
cycles, mopeds, other taxis, sedans, and finally a bus roar past. The leg
lifts slightly and follows the rest of the body into the taxi. Its door shuts.
The driver looks over his shoulder. Everyone, all three of them, are in.
The second taxi, filled with luggage, idles behind them. At the railroad
station—white concrete, uninspiring—the woman enters from the
south, as we have said. The man precedes her. The priest trails behind

the two drivers, helping with the luggage, unaware of what he has witnessed.

"It's raining," the woman says.

"What?"

"Isnt that rain? Look—outside."

A white arm points. The priest has almost bumped into her. Outside a deluge of water roars over the street they have just left. The husband is in an office—he can be seen, bent over a table, while sheets of paper are examined, stamped, signed. The priest blinks his eyes. He runs a hand through his graying hair. Sweat has already darkened his shirt. Luggage—expensive Vuitton, heavy duffles—are around him. He stares at the woman, and then looks outside.

"Ah," he says. "The rain. Have you been in the tropics before?"

"Is that where we are?"

"It must be the rainy season."

The rain eases, and for a moment there is a breeze, almost cool.

"Nice," he says.

"What?"

"This breeze. Though you seem cool enough."

"It's hot though, isnt it. Sticky. Will it be cool where we're going?"

"Cool? I doubt it."

"But air-conditioned, at least?"

"Yes. Well, one can hope, can't one?"

6

There is a slapping sound. Perhaps it is the wheels on the iron tracks. Or perhaps—although this could occur at this point only in the imagination, if at all—it is the sound of one belly slapping against another. Does she imagine the blond man, or the priest, on top of her, slapping away? Do they imagine, either of the men, penetrating her body, sliding their organ rhythmically within her sleek orifice? She is certainly beautiful. The moonlight—the light from what the Maya call pach caae—is cast through the windows of their railroad car. This glow is golden on her face. She sits with her legs pointed into the aisle, one leg crossed over the other. The two men are opposite her in seats which face each other. The seats are leather, the wood dark. The carriage is small. Their luggage is piled to one side. Within the woman's expensive bags are carefully folded dresses, shoes snugly heel-to-toe, and undergarments so flimsy they would rip apart at the merest caress. Later many of these items will be described, and their uses delineated. Outside is a landscape of cavernous trees. That is, the trees are so thick, so blackly green, they have the appearance of deep caves. The train rattles and sways past this dense landscape.

Attached ahead of them is another train carriage—a second-class carriage overfilled with people. The people can be seen dimly illuminated by overhead lights, packed together. Occasionally they press their faces against the glass pane of the door at the end of their carriage. The faces are brown, small, pointed. Teeth are missing from their mouths, and the teeth that are present are often outlined in gold. The eyes are so dark that their pupils cannot be seen. When these eyes turn,

45

just so, toward the light, they pick up a coppery sheen. The faces press against the window pane, then turn and talk volubly. After a while a new face will appear. The eyes in each of these faces shine like polished copper.

Earlier the woman said:

"Does anyone know where we are going?"

"It's marked," the blond man said.

"Marked?"

"On your map."

"Oh." She pretended to study it. "It doesnt make much sense."

"Let me show you." It was the priest. He stood next to her and with a pencil followed a line on the map. "You see? We arrived here. It's the provincial capital. The train—ah, here it is. This way—this way—to here. A small village, I should think."

"Is it far?"

"Given our speed—or our lack of speed—we should arrive tomorrow. Perhaps late."

"Are you an actor?"

"An actor?" He drummed the pencil against his wrist. "An actor. Well, I suppose I am. For this movie, at least. But what I really am— what I really am, you see—is a playwright."

"A playwright?"

"But not a successful one."

He drummed the pencil some more, then abruptly stuck it in his shirt pocket.

"No," he said. "Not a successful one. If you wish to speak of acting you must talk to Garred."

"Garred?"

"Our companion. He is the only professional amongst us, I'm afraid."

She leaned forward and whispered: "Is he angry with me?"

The priest raised his head and blinked his eyes.

"Well," he said softly. "He does seem—well, he does seem angry. But I'm sure—I'm sure, my dear—you neednt take it personally."

"I neednt?"

"Not personally. No, I dont think so. Neither of us."

"This morning I thought he was going to hit me."

"No, no."

"You dont think so?"

"I cant believe—"

"Well," she said. Then she added: "I'm an actress."

"Yes?"

"I was in two movies. I mean, I was supposed to be. I had lines, and everything."

"What happened?"

"My scenes were cut."

"Ah."

"I was never so disappointed. I told all my friends. Can you imagine? And then I'm not there at all."

"Yes, disappointing. I can see that."

"I hope I wont be cut from this one."

"Yes. Yes. We can hope so."

Beyond them, at the window to the next carriage, a face pressed. It was so flattened and distorted by the glass it was not clear if it was a man's face or a woman's. It stared into the carriage, the eyes picking up coppery glints of light .

"Yes," said the priest, eyes vaguely moving. "We can all hope so."

During the day the train stopped at villages. People got on. No one ever seemed to get off. Men, women, children stood alongside the tracks with huge boxes tied with twine and jute sacks stacked one on top of the other. How did they get in? The carriage was already full. Children wailed, women cried out, men shouted. But once the train was moving the track was empty and the wails and cries disappeared beneath the clack of the iron wheels.

"What did you say your name was?"

"Garred Haus."

"Garred Haus! What a funny name. Have I introduced myself?"

"Yes."

"I'm Virginia White. I toured Vietnam with the USO. That country looked just like this. We're not in Vietnam, are we? I wouldn't want to go there again!"

"Never fear, my dear. Were in no country youve ever heard of."

"I mean, I enjoyed my tour. And it was good for my career. But it was so terrible, what happened to our boys there. So terrible, dont you think? And then just to pull out, as though nothing had happened. It's all politics, isnt it? That's what they told me. All those boys—they were so angry. We didnt let them do their job, did we? I mean our politicians didnt. We could have won that war. Our boys could have won it—that's what they all told me. If we had just turned them loose, to do their job."

"It was a nasty war," says the priest.

"Do you know what this movie is about?"

"Havent you read the script?"

"My agent read it. Do I have a good part?"

"Essential."

"You mean it's important? My agent said it was important."

"That's right."

"They wont cut me out in the editing, will they?"

"Not unless they cut everything."

"Good." She smiled. "What is your name? Did we do this before?"

"We introduced ourselves back at the hotel."

"But I've forgotten."

"Osgood Fetters."

"Osgood Fetters!"

"That's right."

"What a strange name!"

"Isnt it?"

7

The night is occluded. The moon—pach caae—is obscured. Rain spatters the window. Earlier, the woman—the one who calls herself Virginia White—wondered aloud about lunch. No one had thought to bring food, and there was clearly no restaurant car on this train. The next time the train stopped, Garred Haus—the "husband"—leaned out a window and, via sign language and a display of currency, acquired what looked like corn tortillas or chapatis folded over a smear of gravy. No one else wanted one, however, so Garred ate them all, wolfishly. Water? There was no water. The bathroom at one end of the carriage— they had to brave the faces pressed against the window to approach it— had a broken tap. The toilet itself was merely a hole in the floor open to the track below. There was a lingering odor within the tiny room of ammonia, and no one, especially the woman, spent any more time within its confines than necessary. The next time the train stopped— more people got on; no one got off—Garred Haus again leaned out the window, and moments later brought forth three bottles of Coca Cola, surely the most ubiquitous liquid in existence. They were tepid and sickly sweet, but wet. The woman wrinkled her nose: Was there no Diet Coke? She took pretty little swallows, as though by drinking so slowly she would imbibe fewer calories.

All this time she is dressed in white. While she is dressed in white the train passes shrubs blossoming with the white plumeria. Sometimes these flowers are so close that Garred Haus, had he so desired, could have plucked one and given it to the woman, who herself—as we shall see—resembles the plumeria. Each blossom—we are speaking now of the flower—has a five-parted calyx. There are five stamens. There are five spreading corolla lobes, or petals, that overlap at their bases, rather like propellers. The lobes have a waxy appearance. The flowers, as well as the succulent branches, which possess large leaves pinnately veined, contain an abundant milky sap that is reputed to be caustic, perhaps even poisonous. The flowers are generally fragrant. They are named after Charles Plumier, a French botanist who died in 1704. The plant, in both shrub and tree form, is found throughout tropical America and the West Indies, where they belong to the dogbane family, and in Hawaii, where they are often used in leis for tourists, who do not understand what they are putting around their necks. They are common also throughout Asia, where they are a favored offering to Buddhist temples, and thus often called the temple flower. The woman Virginia White resembles the plumeria, especially the white plumeria, in the following particulars: her pale skin, translucent and waxy with sweat; the blossom between her legs, whose lobes, or lips, are noticeably waxy from their effulgent secretions and tinged with the same pink often found in the heart of the plumeria; her succulent limbs, veined; her abundant sap, which may or may not be caustic; her fragrance. The flower itself is robust; so too is the woman, although this would be more apparent were she naked. Her flesh, like the thick-petaled plumeria, is firm, well-packed, amply curved, swelling. With one exception this robust body is clothed in garments of exceeding delicacy. The exception is her hose: a one-piece garment which pulls up to her hips, covering her from the tips of her toes to her waist, and named Ironweave Pantihose. This garment is available in supermarkets throughout America and offers protection against mosquitoes and sunburn; it repels water and—because of its rough texture—roving hands. In particular it occludes the woman's sex organ, the waxy lobes of which are flattened by the Ironweave and hidden even more completely than the moon overhead is hidden by clouds. If one saw her clad in this garment, one's first impression would be that she had no orifice, that there was no entrance to her body, no exit. Smooth to the eye, rough to the hand, apertureless, the lower half of her body thus resembles a mannikin, one of those window dummies whose only purpose is to display artifacts for sale.

Her breasts, however—we shall continue this description—are sheathed by a brassiere so fine, so delicate, it is a wonder it can contain her swelling flesh. Through the material is visible the roseate glow of each nipple. Over the brassiere a thin slip falls to mid-thigh; then a translucent blouse tucked into a straight white skirt. On her feet are white pumps with spindly heels at least four inches high. The lips on her face are painted pink and covered with a waxy gloss. They are unrestrained, open, exposed, well-rounded, fleshy, and thus inviting, exactly the opposite of the lips between her legs so crushed by the Ironweave fabric of her hose. It is not clear what one can make of this. Perhaps, in the course of this story, or in the course of the film, we will find out.

In the meantime the night is occluded. Rain slaps against the window panes. The air outside is thick with insects. Within the carriage the three actors prepare uneasily for sleep. Faintly perceived above the clack of the iron wheels are the cries and moans from the people pressed together in the second class carriage. These people stand, sit, lie, flesh to flesh, amongst children half crushed, women seemingly in labor, men wild-eyed with hunger, draped over sacks of dried corn, bags of rice, and chickens gasping in bamboo cages. None of them, we are sure, can sleep this night, unless it is the sleep of the mad: the air filled with perfervid images, contorted dreams, thick fevers. In the smaller carriage the three actors themselves sleep fitfully on their leather seats. None has undressed; only shoes have come off. In the morning the three are noticeably awry. Waterless, they can only pat at their faces, rearrange their wrinkled garments, run brush or fingers through hair still damp from the night's sweats. When the train stops, Garred acquires more Cokes, which restore them somewhat. More people climb on board: withered women, crippled men, children with pus dripping from wounds.

As the train lurches through the lush countryside the woman Virginia White walks—cautiously on her four inch heels—to the cubicle at the end. Dark faces stare at her; lips move rapidly in speech that is not audible; their eyes flash, right and left, with coppery glints.

When she emerges the faces are still there. A fist bangs on the glass pane of the door. The faces twist and turn; their lips distort.

"I think theyre trying to get in," she says. "They cant get in, can they?"

"Our door is locked," says Garred. "I checked it yesterday."

"Perhaps," says the priest, "we could let a few of them—the women—"

"If you let one in, they will all come in. Forget it, priest. They are used to their conditions."

"I'm not a priest."

"Of course not."

Garred Haus reclines on his seat; his feet are up on the seat opposite, in twisted beige socks. His shirt is open to the waist. His eyes are closed. His sallow face is shiny with sweat.

"It's hot," says the woman. "It's already hotter than yesterday."

No one responds. After a while the banging on the window ceases.

8

The northern walls are adobe and painted white. Shortly these walls will come into view. First, however, the train stops at another village. A black limousine is parked there. At its side stands an Oriental man in a visored cap. When the train stops, he comes up to the carriage window.

"Mr Haus? Mr Fetters? Miss White?"

"It seems," says Osgood Fetters, "we have finally arrived."

"Thank God."

The woman's hand, with its pink nails, is at her throat.

"I dont think," she continues, "I could take another minute of this."

They stand by the car. Ragged children drag luggage from the train across the red dirt. These are stacked in the limousine's voluminous trunk; only the last two are tied on top. The Oriental man, who has a round face and a chubby body, opens a door. The three actors fit comfortably in the back seat. As soon as the engine fires, cold air begins to hiss around them. Almost immediately sweat pours down their faces, their torsos, their thighs: their bodies are still producing sweat to cope with the heat experienced outside, but in the cold air the sweat no longer evaporates. Black smears of mascara descend from the woman's eyes. Her thin blouse, already grayish and damp, becomes sopping wet. She gasps, drawing cold air into her lungs. It takes several minutes for their bodies to adjust to this cold. By then they are squirming in their own moisture, the woman especially. It is at this point that Osgood Fetters, perhaps in his role as priest, taps at his window—he is sitting on the right—and says:

"Look!"

"What is it?"

"They're burning something—no, someone—"

Virginia White cranes her neck around, brushing at the sweat in her eyes.

"What is it?" she repeats. "What did you say?"

"That man's on fire!"

The scene the priest refers to is being enacted in an open space surrounded by trees. The limbs of these trees droop low to the ground. Between the ceibas and the red zapotes and the tall balche trees are the plumerias, some of whose blossoms are plum colored, some scarlet, others white. The tallest tree of all is the *Antiaris toxicaria*, or sack tree, whose poisonous sap is often used in punji traps. These trees, within whose cavernous depths roam kinkajous and foxes, swollen iguanas, grouse, even jaguars, form a dense wall around the clearing. Although they possess genuine beauty, they are genuinely foreboding as well. Within the primeval forest are forces which are truly dangerous. The primitive people who live within these forests, and the village people who carve out spaces at their edges, give many names and meanings to these forces. In truth the forces which exist there are embodied in the jungle itself: that is, the plants and animals are themselves those forces exemplified, made visible. They exemplify the urge to life, an urge which is perversely destructive. That is why parasites kill their hosts, why a vine will claw its way over a tree until the tree dies beneath it, why scorpions drip poison, why a spider will kill its mate, why trees exude vile sap and animals devour each other in their mad lust for life. The very fertility of the earth depends upon death: the decomposing carcasses are themselves the humors of life. It is in this context that we must witness the events in the clearing which our three actors are now passing. Plunging from the trees—out of the darkness—is a crane with a giant Panavision camera mounted at its tip. It rises drunkenly from the shadows, and then swoops low over the ground. At its base stand men in jungle fatigue pants and T-shirts. Across the clearing are fifty to sixty people, some of them in the orange robes of Buddhist monks. Several are dancing; their robes swirl around their sandaled feet. In front of them is a gray car, perhaps a French Simca, or an English Hillman, with its hood, or bonnet, raised. To one side is a five gallon can of the type used to carry gasoline. In the center of the clearing is the man himself, the Thich, or Venerable, Quang Duc, or his simile. His hands are in his lap. He sits lotus fashion. Around him swirl—rather like the orange robes of the dancing monks—ochre flames. These flames are deceptively light—insubstantial, translucent, perhaps soundless, although this must be uncertain from within the limousine. Nevertheless they are fierce enough to turn the Venerable Quang Duc's skin—or his simile's skin—black. The skin peels. A darkish smoke, an oily smoke, appears around the flames, whose density perhaps increases. When a wind blows aside the flames, an expression of ineffable pain can be glimpsed on the Venerable's face.

"That man's burning to death!"

"Dont be a fool, Fetters."

"No—the skin peeling—my God, those eyes—"

"Remember where you are, man. This is movieland. Nothing is real."

They have passed the clearing. The way is rutted, and tree limbs occasionally brush the top of the limousine.

"No, that was real—he looked—"

"Looked, Fetters. Seemed. Actors will burn their Equity cards, but not themselves. Not even for a percentage of the gross."

"I swear—"

"Take hold of yourself, man."

"It looked so real!"

"Good. Perhaps this production isnt as half-assed as it seems."

The woman, who sits between the two men, stares from one to the other. Garred Haus has scarcely stirred; it is not clear he even looked at the burning figure. Osgood Fetters at last falls back into his seat, although his face remains pale.

The woman claps her hands together. "My goodness!" she says. "This is exciting!"

Soon the white adobe walls, as we have promised, come into view. The building is surrounded by trees and shrubs. The air is darkish, damp.

Osgood Fetters comments that the building looks like a church. The woman, still on the edge of her seat, agrees. The car stops to the north, where a path begins. Garred Haus watches suspiciously—the lid of his right eye lowered—while the Oriental man unties the two pieces of luggage. He carries these two pieces—quick short steps, as though he were walking in Japanese sandals—ahead of the three actors, down the path, between chacah and chulul, past homa gourds and scorpion trees, yellow kan-lol and hanging pupae, to the white door set between the adobe walls. The oriental man immediately announces—as he pushes the door open—that he speaks no English. Perhaps he has announced this to forestall questions. Nevertheless Garred speaks. German? he suggests. French? Spanish? *Hungarian?* No English, repeats the Oriental man. He puts the two pieces of luggage down inside the door and scurries away. The three actors go inside. They move from display case to display case. What is this? the woman asks. Terra-cotta, Osgood answers promptly. There is obsidian and carved limestone, ceramics and jade, both inside the cases and fastened to the walls. Osgood Fetters puts glasses onto the bridge of his nose, and stoops low, sniffing. These look like pustules, he says, smallpox pustules. Although I suppose—and what is this? Pretty, dont you think? What do they call it? Not ceramic—er—mosaic, thats it, a mosaic jade mask. And look at the ruby eyes—well, theyre probably glass—in that jaguar.

Garred leaves the room. When he returns, his hands are stuck in his pockets. He watches the man and the woman.

"Where's the chink?" he says finally.

"The Oriental—uh—gentleman?"

"That's the one."

"Well—"

Garred walks past Osgood Fetters, whose eyes are blinking behind his spectacles, and goes outside. Some moments later he returns with a duffle over one shoulder.

"Better do something about your luggage," he says.

"Our luggage?"
"It's piled on the road."
"What do you mean?"
"It's piled on the road."
"But that man—"
"The chink's gone."

9

The cenote lies in the center of the building: the exact center of the building, directly beneath the dome which rises perhaps forty meters overhead. Although we are given to understand that this building is a reproduction, that it was built recently for the purpose, specifically, of this film, we are suspicious. It looks old. More importantly, it feels old. It has that deep darkness, that ancient weight, that only an old building can possess. Moreover, around one side of the cenote is what must be centuries of accumulated bat guano. Would a movie company be so interested in verisimilitude as to import bat guano? Living in the bat guano are fungi, specifically the *Bacillus subtilis* Cohn and *Bacillus mycoides* Flugge, of the order Eubacteriales. These fungi are phototactic, capable of fruiting when light is entirely absent, and can rapidly decompose proteinaceous materials. The cenote itself is actually a cave, as are all cenotes, in this case of the two-cycle solution type, which is indicated by its irregular, reticulate form and the presence— perhaps we shall discover these later—of high-vaulted chambers. There is a considerable pool of water perhaps ten meters, or about thirty-three feet, below the irregular surface. Doubtless because of the presence of this large body of water, the air temperature in the center of this building will vary only between 23.2 and 27.9 degrees Celsius, with the humidity maintained over 90%. Within this cenote and around its edge live troglophile, troglobite and occasionally trogloxene animals. Some authorities (Arndt, 1923; Mohr, 1928) name these creatures troglobitic, troglophilic, ombrophilic and euryphotic, while others (Gebhard, 1932; Kolsavary, 1934) prefer the terms eutroglobionts, hemitroglobionts, pseudotroglobionts, tychotroglobients, and additionally, troglocheimadas. In any case, many of these creatures, however they are classified, are blind, colorless, hydrophylic. There are rhabdocoeis and triclads, rhyizopods and ciliates, several varieties of nematodes, simple polychaetes, oligochaetes, leeches, rotifers, pulmonate and prosobranch snails, sphaerid clams, many cave crustaceans such as cladocerans and copepods, including parasitic species, archaid anispidaceans, several aquatic and terrestrial isopods, many amphipods and palaemonid shrimps, arachnids such as aquatic and terrestrial mites, ticks, many spiders, pseudoscorpions, whip scorpions, scorpions, millipedes and centipedes, thysanurans and collembolans, psocids and earwigs, cockroaches, phasmids, beetles, dipterans, and cave crickets. In the water itself are fish such as the amblyopsid, the silurid, some cyprinids, brotulids, and symbranchid eels. The amphibians are chiefly salamanders, both aquatic and terrestrial, often with degenerate eyes. The troglophiles include lizards and snakes. Many of these creatures are blind, but are recompensed with unusually effective tactile and olfactory organs. Their bodies may be pale and pellucid, without pigment; small, stenothermic; and hydrophylic. Many of the fish, and some of the crustaceans, are luminescent. The silurids have long tactile and gustatory barbels on their heads. The bats are nocturnal and feed largely without using their organs of vision; some, in fact, have degenerate eyes. The cave crickets subsist entirely on the remains of insects in the bat feces. Many of the other creatures we have named feed also on the organic remains found in the guano, which is fecund. Other creatures simply eat each other. We shall deal more specifically with some of them, and the details of their lives, later.

The building, as we have said, resembles a fat cross. The three actors sleep in the red room. The red room comprises the eastern arm. It lies precisely on that cardinal direction. The northern room is the white-painted adobe room, filled with artifacts. At this hour it is empty of people, if not of other creatures. The surface of the cenote is occasionally disturbed by movements of schizopods, sphaeromids, cirolanids, amphipods, blind brotulid and amblyopsid fish. The sleep of our actors is disturbed also. None of them can be comfortable. For the woman and the priest, this is their first night, ever, beneath the shroud of a mosquito net. The room, of course, is filled with both anopheline and aedene mosquitoes; the former carry malaria, the latter yellow fever. The "beds" on which these actors sleep are no more than burlap stretched over wooden frames. There are no sheets. Blankets are not needed in this heat. There is no movement of air, although the windows in the room are all open. Even if the air did move, the mosquito nets would largely prevent the air from sliding over, and thus cooling, the skin of our sleeping actors. Garred Haus, the husband, lies in a pair of bikini underpants. Osgood Fetters, the priest, lies in boxer shorts and singlet. The woman Virginia White has troubled to change into pajamas. When she tosses from side to side—which she does often, half awake—her breasts, loose, unconstrained, flow beneath her pajama tops like waves moving the surface of the sea .

10

There is a drop of blood on her arm. The blood—a single drop—appears when the woman scratches a mosquito bite. She is still in her pajamas, which are decorated with small figures of an anthropomorphic rodent called "Mickey Mouse," a creation of the American entrepreneur Walt Disney. This creature has that wide, idiotic smile, that maniacally cheerful innocence, which Americans feel is their patrimony. On her feet are "bunny slippers." On her bed, still shrouded by netting, is the "teddy bear" with whom she slept the night. Is this possible? Are we exaggerating? Can we believe that this grown woman, who must be more than thirty years old, even if she looks younger, would travel with, or even possess, Mickey Mouse pajamas and bunny slippers and a teddy bear? This morning, despite scratching blood from one of many mosquito bites, despite being tousled, smudged, unwashed, this woman sits sleepy-eyed on the edge of her bed, feet and legs together, hands on knees, a bright smile on her face, like a child expecting applause or perhaps a trip to the zoo.

Last night she was not so cheerful. She and Osgood Fetters rushed out to the road. Halfway there, Fetters suddenly faltered, a grimace on his face. What is it? the woman said, pausing. Are you all right? It's nothing, he answered, just a muscle cramp. He did not know it, but a blood vessel had burst deep within the calf muscle of his right leg. In a few days the leg would be swollen and blackly bruised. Now, however, slowly, carefully, he hobbled to the road where their luggage, indeed, was piled.

He brought in one suitcase, then another. She carried two at a time, wobbling on her high heels. He made more journeys, in obvious pain. The woman's face was dusty and tight-lipped. They piled their luggage inside the door. Garred Haus was nowhere in sight. At last they found him in the "red room," which was apparently where they were all expected to sleep. Garred had already selected his bed there, the largest, and was reclining on it, smoking one of his Gauloises. The woman and the priest then carried their luggage into this room, one and two at a time, past the artifacts, past the cenote, past the bat guano. The woman's white clothes were filthy. She plunked herself down on her "bed." Her mouth pushed open and shut like the mouth of a fish taken from water.

"What," she said, "is going on here?"

Although the question was rather tossed out into the air, it was actually addressed to Garred, who ignored it.

"I have never been so despicably treated."

Garred blew smoke into the air.

"I am going to complain," she announced, "to the producer."

Osgood Fetters had put his leg up and was massaging the calf.

"We shall all complain," he said, as though he were capable of speaking for Garred. "This is intolerable. You're quite right."

"No one should have to put up with this."

"No one."

"This isnt a movie; it's a torture chamber."

"Exactly."

"This isnt even a hotel."

"It's not even a decent dormitory."

"Am I supposed to sleep on one of these things?"

She banged at the burlap, from which rose a cloud of dust.

"Where's my shower? Where's my bathroom? I want my own bedroom. We need a cook—someone to do our clothes—decent accommodations—"

"Hear, hear."

"I wont put up with this. I simply wont."

"Youre quite right."

"I simply," she repeated, "wont put up with this."

She then sat there, looking around, as though expecting something to happen.

After a while she pushed out her lower lip and began to sniff. No one noticed. Garred, droopy-eyed, was blowing smoke into the air. Osgood, pant leg pulled up, was still massaging his calf.

She whimpered, softly; then again, more loudly.

Osgood leaped up.

"My dear!" he said.

He limped to her side and put an arm around her.

"Are you quite all right?"

"No," she said, suddenly gasping with sobs. "No, I'm not all right. I'm filthy, I'm all dirty, I cant do my hair, I feel ugly—"

"My dear!"

"Nothing is going right, nothing ever goes right, I dreamed of this, I dreamed all my life, and now look at me, a filthy mess!"

"My dear!"

"It's not right! It's just not right!"

"Here, here now!"

"It's not fair!"

"My dear, surely, tomorrow all this—"

"I dont *care* about tomorrow! It's not right *now*! Tomorrow will be just as horrible! I know it!"

"No, no, really—youll see—"

"I dont see! I dont want to see! I dont want to see any of this!"

"My dear! My dear!"

She buried her head on his shoulder.

Yet the evening, and the night, passed, as we have indicated. There was a five gallon bottle of water mounted on a swivel base, allowing its contents to be poured into a chipped enamel cup. On a shelf were three tins of tuna fish and two papayas. There was an outside toilet of sorts, a dank, smelly shed, more like a simple outhouse than a bathroom. The woman used it, almost in tears, peeling down her Ironweave Pantihose, letting out a discreet fart and then a dribble of shit. The toilet paper came from Garred, who alone seemed prepared for these eventualities. Garred had put a bucket of water just outside the door for washing. The bucket had a long rope attached, and the water came from the cenote itself. The bar of soap was Garred's, of course. The woman, used to American motels which supplied everything, carried no soap with her, although in her luggage she had two brands of shampoos, three different hair conditioners, a mouth wash, and sundry other items of personal hygiene, including what must have been a year's supply of tampons. Garred showed her and Osgood Fetters how the mosquito nets worked, which was simple enough, and they crawled under them as the sun—kinich-kach-moo—fell below the horizon and the mosquitoes rose from their fetid pools and shadowy lairs to take over the night.

But morning comes. The dawn then is as rosy as a woman's—as Virginia White's—cheeks, and all seems possible again, even if you are perched on the edge of a burlap-covered bed. Her blubbery lower lip now retracted, sleepy-eyed but pert, clothed in her infantile pajamas and bunny slippers, as charming as a well-behaved twelve-year-old, the American woman Virginia White is ready for anything.

Nothing happens. They dine on a papaya—the Swiss army knife comes from Garred's duffle—and take turns sipping at the enameled cup. At nine o'clock Garred announces he will walk to town. He collects a few dollars from each of the others ("Diet Coke, please") and immediately leaves. His absence creates an odd stillness in the room. The two remaining people, the "priest" Osgood Fetters, with his sore leg, and the "wife" Virginia White, in her Mickey Mouse pajamas, stare at each other across the room.

═══ 11 ═══

In her luggage the woman has several white dresses, plus white skirts and blouses. Many of the blouses are embroidered. Some have what are called Peter Pan collars. There are also frail white brassieres, white panties, white slips and camisoles, white shoes, and several pair of white Ironweave Pantihose. There is clothing in other colors, too; we will describe some of them later. But for today she wears only the rodent pajamas and the bunny slippers. Osgood Fetters is doubtless aware of the looseness of her breasts beneath her torso. She certainly is. When she walks, when she shifts her torso, these breasts seem to move independently, swinging right and left, up and down, whichever way they please. But a woman could hardly be accused of seductiveness or overt sexuality in Mickey Mouse pajamas and bunny slippers, could she? Could anything be more innocent? She chats with a kind of childish happiness of her career, her upbringing in Iowa, her boyfriends back home, her dream of being a famous actress. Osgood, a bit donnish, a gentle man—he should really have a pipe in his mouth—encourages her expansiveness. His avuncular air, combined with her innocence, allows her—rather perversely, we are afraid—to swing her breasts more than necessary, and to frequently cross and uncross her legs, as though her cunt itched, and to coquettishly pat at her hair—to flirt, in fact, the way a little girl will flirt with a favored uncle. It is all quite innocent, and thus allowed, surely. The two of them stroll through the garden outside, Osgood limping, the woman plucking flowers, including the ic-bac nicte, or Little Girl Plumeria. Neither of them notice the locusts or scorpions, the xulab or the chac uaya-cab, or the hanging pupae. The sunlight is warm, the air reasonably dry. Beyond the road rise the giant trees of the forest. There are hills on three sides, all deeply forested. The air is quite still, awaiting developments. When they go back inside, the woman places the flowers around the room in bottles and tin cans. That seems more cheerful, she says, and Osgood agrees. He has been talking now of his career—rather, his failures—as a playwright; and with this charming girl, in this place, with the sun just so, his failures seem, even to him, amusing. He tells anecdotes of producers who chewed cigars, of method actors who chewed lines, of the amateur groups (housewives from Queens, gay men aging into their toupees) who did put on his plays, and the resulting discomfort of their audiences, who under stood nothing. He chuckles over the despairing jobs he held on the fringes of the theatre world, of waiting tables, clerking at hotels, at last finding a more-or-less stable part-time job with a law firm, writing briefs and other missives. The two lawyers for whom he worked seemed relieved to have someone who could make their presentations sound suitably, correctly opaque, yet someone who could adorn their letters with an occasionally lucid sentence. Osgood's mastery of legalese was quick and easy—writing is writing, after all—and he amused himself within its constraints with subtle turns of phrases, with lines in iambic pentameter, with obscure echoes of Eugene Ionesco and Samuel Beckett. Things no one but him, he was sure, would be aware of.

Thus the morning passed pleasantly enough. For lunch Osgood opened a tin of tuna, using Garred's Swiss knife, only cutting himself once. The woman wished, wistfully, for tea, Osgood for gelata and a good expresso. The afternoon passed with more strain. Perhaps the woman's role as child was beginning to weigh on her. How cheerful can one be, when there is no trip to the zoo in the offing? no tea? no finger sandwiches? no boyfriends? no admiring glances from passing strangers? no full-length mirrors in which to admire oneself? no stores in which to shop? no bedrooms to adorn with teddy bears and other anthropomorphic creatures? no hot water for a bath? no tub for a bath? no television "talk-shows?" no music to set her feet atwinkling? no car to drive? no telephone with which to hold long, chirping, cheerful conversations with girlfriends? And besides, Osgood was stumbling now over his anecdotes, which were becoming morose and boring. There was an embarrassed look about him, too, a bit of lustful confusion, guilty desire—her breasts had apparently gotten to him—which she did not find amusing. Uncles were supposed to know their roles, after all. But that was the trouble with men. They were infuriatingly incapable of taking her innocent display—she meant nothing by it— in the spirit in which it was offered. At least, with his injured leg, she could evade him if this became necessary. But his tumescence was discomfiting. She sat straightly on the edge of her bed, and buttoned one more button of her pajama top. Mickey Mouse would defend her.

But at last a battered car comes up the road, blowing steam and leaking water. Garred Haus gets out with two jute sacks. He carries them with deceptive ease—they are actually quite heavy—through the white room, past the cenote and the bat guano, into the red room. There he finds Osgood Fetters and Virginia White in the attitudes we have described. The woman becomes immediately animated. Osgood hunches his shoulders, as though trying to hide. Garred unloads from his sacks two sixpacks of Cokes—no Diet Cokes, no diet anything, no one in that country is on a diet—more tins of tuna, a can of kerosene, a pressure-type lantern, two bottles of rum, three bottles of Chinese brandy, mosquito coils, two long loaves of crusty bread, mangoes, papayas, a pineapple, a bunch of bananas, and two more tin cups, one of which he immediately fills with Coke and a healthy slug of rum. Young Virginia claps her hands, breasts swinging again. Somehow the top button of her pajamas has unbuttoned itself. Garred takes his cup to his bed and starts fishing out a cigarette from his crumpled pack. "They are behind schedule," he says. *All* movies were behind schedule .They were shooting a scene when he reached town: GIs marching through the street with crowds cheering and girls throwing flowers. Garred does not go into detail. The girls, however, *we* understand, were bar girls imported especially for this scene. They were suspended in gilt cages above the street. They threw flower *petals*—the waxy lobes of the plumeria—onto the marching GIs, but first they rubbed the petals on their pussies. "Hey, GI! You want fuckee-fuckee? You want suck pussy? You come to mama-san, baby! I suckee-fuckee good time boy!" Pulling plumeria petals redolent of their effulgent secretions from their bikini bottoms, tossing them, watching them float serenely onto the upturned faces and opened mouths of the young soldiers. The GIs cheered, or the extras playing GIs cheered, marching down the street in one direction, then turning and marching back up it. "More flowers!" someone yelled. "Get those girls more flowers!" The girls plucked at their own teats and rubbed their famous pussies against the bars of their gilded cages.

"I dont remember," Osgood says from across the room, after clearing his throat, "any GIs in the script."

"We only have part of the script."

"Yes, I know. But soldiers—there's nothing there about soldiers. I mean, there's no place in the story for soldiers—"

"Scripts change, Fetters."

"Yes, surely. But—"

"Soldiers are popular now in America, arent they?"

"Yes, but in Yucatan?"

"What difference does it make?"

"I know scripts—I write them. You cant just stick in some extraneous element—I mean, for no reason—"

"This is the movies, Fetters."

"Yes, surely. But—"

"Anything can happen."

"I dont understand. I just dont understand these soldiers."

"Wait," says the woman, who has been staring back and forth at the two, rather like a spectator following the ball at a tennis match. "What about us? Did you talk to anyone about us?"

"Someone's coming for us tomorrow."

What the man—he was identified to Garred as the Assistant Director—actually said was, "Just stay cool, buddy. Someone'll getcha tomorra, okay?" He was a tall man, a bit gone to seed, a hard man turning soft in a sweat-stained T-shirt and jungle fatigue pants. A duckbill cap was pushed back on his head. His accent was southern American, bayou country, Louisiana maybe, juicy like a swamp. He had eyes with hardly any color. He pushed Garred out of the way—put his hand flat on Garred's chest and just shoved a little, hardly any effort, moving aside a minor irritation—and stalked off to some obscure duty, perhaps to get flowers for the bar girls. There was a .45 pistol stuck in his back pocket. Garred wandered through the crowd. He talked to a lighting man holding big aluminum reflectors, a key grip in a floppy hat, an assistant cameraman who tried to bum cigarettes from him. When the street scene, the marching GIs, was finished, close-ups began: closeups of the suckee-fuckee girls, close-ups of GI faces, a snatch of dialog repeated from three different angles, an aluminum reflector here, another there, diffusion screen overhead ("Get rid of that shadow!"), interminable waits while everything was put together, while sound men swore and cameramen snapped. It was all melee. In the confusion Garred slipped from group to group, Gauloise smouldering, listening.

He tells little of this to Osgood Fetters and Virginia White. We ourselves will not repeat the conversations he had or the fragments he overheard. Some of the information contained in them will become apparent shortly. For some time he sat in a dark little store. It was owned by an elderly Chinese. Garred sipped beer and watched the afternoon wane. Finally he acquired all the items we have mentioned. The Chinaman himself—his shop, small as it was, contained canned Lychee nuts from Shanghai and rodent poison from America, Tiger Balm from Singapore and White Horse Whiskey from Canada—supplied most of it and sent out for the rest. He also summoned the car, the local "taxi," and provided the jute sacks and two boys to carry them. All was paid for with a fine sheath of local currency, which Garred had acquired, presciently, in the provincial capital .

Garred stuck his thumb towards the open door of the shop.

"What you think?" he asked.

"Ah," said the Chinese. He touched a finger to his eye. "I look. I see. I say nothing."

"Wise old bird, arent you?"

"Yes, yes, very wise old bird indeed!"

He chuckled. Garred got into the car.

The woman wears a white dress. First, however, she bathes. She is adamant. She will not meet the director, perhaps the producer, perhaps the producer's *girlfriend*, without shampooing her hair and washing her body and putting on fresh clothing, that is, a clean white dress, a red leather belt, and red high-heeled shoes. Her bath is arranged in the following way. The bucket is brought back to the cenote, which is where Garred originally found it. He tosses it into the water thirty-three feet below, drags it full, and hauls it back up. She dips her hair into it—the hair is long, fullbodied, and rather tangled now—and, humming, spends several minutes lathering it. She wears a cotton robe and thong sandals. When the lather has risen to her specifications, Garred pours the bucket over her bent head. "Oooh!" she cries happily. Garred brings up more water. She rubs conditioner into the wet hair. After one minute Garred pours again. He pours a second time. Finally he brings up another bucket and leaves. She is ready now to bathe, a more private act.

Only we shall watch. The two men are in the white room, the door closed. The woman stands naked at the edge of the cenote, in a spot clear of bat guano. The door to the red room, the room which faces east, which faces into the rising sun, is open. Some light comes through this door. Because it comes from only one direction—the center of the building is otherwise quite dark—and because the light is faint, she is deeply shadowed. Her breasts are illuminated on one side, and dark on the other. The hollow of her belly, as she stands at an angle, is shadowed. Her swelling mound of Venus, however, glistens—the pubic hair is wet and each drop of water shines like a diamond. As she turns, pouring cups of water over herself, light illuminates her cleft rump, then one swelling breast, then another. As she soaps herself she continues to turn. Perhaps it is best if we see her from a distance, from near the top of the domed ceiling, for instance, where the bats are hanging. From that distance she is a marionette turning, turning, turning below. Her hands can be seen moving over her robust body. Each breast is given attention. Each thigh is soaped. The light from the door of the red room functions exactly as a spotlight would function. She turns in this spotlight. Her head falls back, exposing her throat. When both breasts are turned into the light she lifts them, one hand to each breast, as though offering them to an audience. Each breast is rinsed individually. All this time she is humming into this vast, dark room. All this time her wet hair hangs, sometimes down her back, sometimes across one shoulder, sometimes, as she turns, and turns, across one breast. All this time she is alone, except for the sleeping bats, except for the silurids in the water below, except for the crickets in the guano and the whip scorpions, false scorpions, and scorpions living beneath the lip of the cenote.

She dresses. She pulls on, awkwardly, white Ironweave Pantihose. She slips her small feet into the red shoes with high, high heels. A brassiere is strapped around her breasts. It is so delicate, a man's hand, stroking a breast through this brassiere, would tear the fabric. She puts on a white cotton dress, a shirtwaist, buttoned down the front and collared. Buttons are left undone so that the thin, delicate brassiere, and the flesh beneath it, may be glimpsed. In the white room she props a mirror on a display case—it contains a terracotta balam, or jaguar—and makes up her face: mascara and eyeliner, a touch of color on the cheekbones, red thickly on the lips, then covered with gloss so the lips are wet, lubricated, inviting. Into the mirror she smiles. She touches her collar. She shifts her breasts, slightly. She is perfect.

Slowly, delicately, perfectly, balanced exactly on her high heels, she returns to the red room to wait.

══ 13 ══

She wears a white dress. It is the dress we have described. She is clean and shining. Gradually however she begins to wilt. The heat becomes stultifying. She sits and sweats. There is no wind. No one comes for them. Breathing itself becomes difficult. The flowers outside droop like open mouths. There is no escape from this heat, which today lies heavily on the red earth.

In the afternoon Garred walks through this heat back to the town. Within the town he finds two slinking dogs, some iguanas and geckos, and ravens pecking at unidentifiable carcasses. Yesterday's flower petals—already brown, already rotting—lie in the street. Many of the buildings are false fronts, apparently constructed just for the scene Garred witnessed the day before. The gilt cages lie behind them, some on their sides. A musky odor hangs there, rather like the perfume of a woman who has just left a room. Garred sniffs, lips peeled back, teeth together: it is the face of a feral animal. He bangs on doors. The Chinaman's shop is shuttered. The train station, the only concrete building in the town, is deserted. The tracks are hot and already rusting. He finds a metal rod there and uses it to pry open a window to the Chinaman's store. The shelves are bare, except for a pile of jute sacks. When the shadows lengthen, he starts back. He finds the other two in the red room. The woman wears the white dress. A red belt is around her waist. On her feet are red shoes with high, high heels. Her legs are crossed at the ankles. The priest is bony and thin. His leg, propped up before him, is now swollen. Bruising is visible. Garred explains what he has seen. There were things he did not tell them yesterday. People yesterday talked nervously of an attempt against the government. There were rumors of a coup. Something like that, he says, must have occurred. The movie company, in any case, had deserted them, perhaps unavoidably. The villagers themselves were gone, although they were possibly hiding in the hills. Perhaps the town lay on the route of an invading army. Perhaps the government had forcibly removed them. Who could say? Luckily they were provisioned for several days. They had fruit, water, canned fish. He himself was fond of Chinese brandy, a taste he had acquired some years before, in Bangkok. There were worse places to be marooned. In a few days the coup would either succeed or fail. The villagers would return; possibly even the movie company. The trains would run, perhaps the buses, perhaps they could hire a car and drive to the provincial capital. Garred lights two mosquito coils: it has grown dark. He fires up the pressure lantern. He peels himself a mango—the juice dribbles down his chin as he eats it—and pours a cup of brandy. In the meanwhile, he says, they could pass the time by practicing their lines. If the movie resumed they would be ready.

"What do you think, Fetters?"

"It seems we have little choice."

"And you, my dear?"

"I dont know what to say."

"We are agreed, then. Brandy, Fetters? Miss White? Or do you prefer rum and Coke?"

14

She wears a white dress. She sprawls on her bed. Her face has that slackness that one sees in drunks or in people deeply, exhaustedly asleep. The room is quite dark; the lantern has gone out. Fortunately the mosquito coils are still glowing: only Osgood Fetters, in singlet and shorts, has crawled under his netting. Garred Haus, shirtless, the top button of his fly undone, snores softly. There is no moon, or if there is a moon, it is entirely obscured by clouds. The only illumination comes from the tracer bullets arcing overhead and the occasional flare which drifts onto the hills from the east. The weapons firing these bullets make rattling, sputtering, and popping sounds. These weapons are a mixture of M-16s, M-14s, AK-47s, CAR-15s, 9mm automatics, .45 automatics, Swedish-Ks, M-60s, ZPM-2s, and an occasional Stoner 63 A1 MK23. After a while mortars, Mark 18 grenade launchers, and RPGs open up—from both sides, both east and west—and then, waking Garred at last, the whine and thump of incoming 105s.

He stares out the window. He puts a cigarette in his mouth but doesnt light it. His sweaty face glows; his eyes droop. When he sees figures moving from the tree line, he goes to Osgood and shakes him awake. "Get under your bed," he orders. Bullets begin to splat against the walls of the building. One whines into the room. Garred rolls Virginia White off her bed onto the tile floor. He lies on top of her. When she tries to speak, he slaps her. By now footsteps are audible outside. Voices flutter past, rather like the wings of bats: dry rustling noises in the dark. A weapon—it is an AK-47, its sound is quite distinctive—goes pop-pop-pop just outside the window. Garred uses this moment to pull open the woman's bodice. A button pops. One brassiere cup, as delicate as we have indicated, rips quite away. Only the underwire remains intact, and this has the effect of pushing her breast up and out, into the mouth which Garred lowers. Once the plump nipple is in his mouth—in better light we would have glimpsed the roseate bud—he begins to bite and suck. It takes a moment for the woman to react. Then she tries to push his head away. The mouth, however, is locked onto her teat. She twists beneath him. A face, meanwhile, appears at a window, looks quickly right and left, somehow misses the figures squirming on the floor, and ducks away. A mortar shell lands just outside. People breathe heavily as they race past. The woman likewise is panting. Garred has left her breast. He is pulling and tugging and jerking at the Ironweave Pantihose, which is as unyielding as jute. The woman's legs are flying in the air. One shoe comes off, and spins across the room. The exposed breast—it is quite lovely in the sporadic light from the tracers—rolls and heaves while the other remains confined within its delicate lace cup. All the while bullets pock-pock-pock against the walls. Occasionally a tracer spins eerily into the room, sizzling like meat on a fire. Osgood Fetters peers out from under his bed. "Garred!" he whispers. "What are you doing?" Garred is still pulling at the Ironweave, while the woman twists and kicks beneath him. "Garred! Are you crazy?" Osgood crawls out from under his bed. A mortar shell explodes outside, sending shrapnel skittering through the room. Osgood ducks back. In any case, it is too late. The Ironweave has been peeled off of one leg, and hangs now about the ankle of the other. The red high-heeled shoe remains somehow on that foot, kicking into the air. The shroud of the pantihose flaps about like an injured animal. Garred rises triumphantly over her—what superhuman effort he has expended!—and plunges into her body. His organ unerringly finds her orifice, like a ferret slipping into its hole. She bucks and twists, but he has impaled her. He rises over her like a lizard. His eyes—they reflect the red light of the tracers—glow like the eyes of a lizard. He thumps, thumps, thumps away at her, while mortars and 105s thump, thump, thump at the hills outside. Osgood crawls over the tile. "Garred! Garred! Youre crazy!"

Garred swings an arm. His backhand catches Osgood in the face.
  "Wait your turn, priest!"
  People garbed in black race past, making sounds like the wings of
bats. After a while they are gone. A few more tracers arc overhead. An
M-60 opens up, briefly. Then everything is quiet. Only smells remain:
cordite, burnt flesh, singed air, semen.

15

The husband stands at the edge of the cenote. It may be that he has no fear of the darkness. He is naked. He seems wiry in this light, the light that comes through the door of the white room. His body is striated with muscle. Only his belly is soft. He pours a bucket of water over himself, then another, dragging it up from the cenote. He shakes himself—he seems almost to growl—and then pulls his pants on over his wet body.

Outside the air is thick from a recent rain. The earth swells, the way a sponge will swell when dipped into sea water. Steam rises from the earth. This rich effluvium is palpable. It is as pungent as the farts of old men, as acrid as the scut of the balam, as sour as old urine. The red plumerias, the scarlet plumerias, the white-petaled plumerias exude an odor as dense as oil. The air itself is as dense as oil. Through this turgid air banks an F-4 Phantom, its engines throttled back. It moves very slowly. It seems almost to pause as it banks away from the eastern hills. The pilot, goggled and masked, is visible through his plexiglass cockpit. As he passes overhead the shriek of his engines causes the woman to rise on her burlap bed. Her movements are sluggish. Across from her, head sunk into his hands, sits the man we call the priest. Visible through the windows are small boys scurrying across the open spaces and along the edges of the hills, putting brass shell casings into jute sacks. The F-4 floats slowly past once more, this time leaving behind an ochre burst of napalm. The woman at last comes upright. She pulls her bodice over the one breast which has lain exposed. Her left eye is blackened. Her lips are bruised. Along the wall nearby moves a swollen iguana—a ppuppulni-huh—which has found its way in from the garden. Through the open door leading to the cenote comes Garred, the husband. Following him are scorpions, false scorpions, whip scorpions, and other insects which will be named. He smacks them with his shoe and piles their carcasses together. Although he has just washed, he is already oily with sweat. So is the woman, who raises her head.

"Why are you angry with me."

"I'm not angry."

"You hit me."

"You never listen to me."

"Tell me what you want."

"If only you would put yourself in my hands."

He has lit his Gauloise. Smoke drifts upward, past his sweating face, past his colorless eyes, past the dank hair lying on his forehead. The tip of his cigarette glows with the same ochre color as the napalm spreading itself on the hills outside. In this turgid air only the smoke moves, rising upward from the corners of his mouth.

"What are you staring at?"

There is no response.

"What are you staring at?"

There is no response.

"What are you staring at?"

"Nothing," she says at last. "I am staring at nothing."

PART THREE

======= 1 =======

Garred rushes off the set. There is no ready explanation for his behavior. A wardrobe woman tries to stop him—his toupee has come loose—but he brushes past her. "Coo," she says. "Aint 'e the one?" Meanwhile, an SP-2H Neptune drones overhead. It carries a Night Observation Scope, AN/PQ-92 Search Radar, FLIR and LLLTV Sensors, Side Looking Airborne Radar, Real Time IR Sensors, Moving Target Indicators, Digital Integrated Attack and Navigation Equipment, and a Black Crow Truck Ignition Sensor. It is armed with twin 20mm cannons in its tail, several miniguns, a 40mm grenade launcher, 500-pound general purpose bombs, and incendiary weapons. It is a lovely sight unloading its weaponry on its digitally displayed targets. There is a kind of serenity to the sight. The Neptune moves slowly. Its LLLTV sensors, its AN/PQ-92s, its Moving Target Indicators pick out, with delectable delicacy, the warm bodies hiding below, moving or not, the truck engines, ignited or not, and the children, alive or not. No one can escape the Night Observation Scope or the Side Looking Airborne Radar. No one can evade the Digital Integrated Attack and Navigation Equipment. Tracer bullets stream from the tail and the miniguns. At the touch of a button 500-pound bombs and incendiaries tumble out, unerringly finding their targets. *Red were the beards of the children of the sun, the bearded ones from the east, when they arrived here in our land. The strangers to the land are white men, red men. There is a beginning of carnal sin. Oh Itza! Make ready. There comes a white circle in the sky, the fair-skinned boy from heaven. Fire shall flame up at the tips of their hands.* Meanwhile, the woman and the man—the ones we call Virginia White

85

and Osgood Fetters—have strolled to the yellow, or southern, room of the cross-shaped building. He shows her a figure carved in wood. It is reclining. It is full sized, that is, as large as a living person. The face is blissfully suffering. Is that possible? The expression on the face reveals both suffering and bliss. There are terrible wounds on this figure. The woman wrinkles up her nose. "Ugh," she says, "that's disgusting." She refers to the roll of intestines visible in the abdominal wound. Black blood has flowed from this wound and crusted at its edges. The black blood has flowed from the wounds on the knees, on the feet, on the hands, on the head. These wounds are depicted in great detail. "It was carved by the Indians 200 years ago," says Osgood, referring to a pamphlet. "It's supposed to be the Christ, of course. But the Indians claim it is really a statue of Jacinto Canek." "Who?" "Jacinto Canek. A rebel, apparently. Caught and executed by the Spanish." Canek was captured following the Maya rebellion of 1761, which he led. His followers were hung, then disemboweled, and pieces of their bodies sent to outlying villages. Jacinto himself was tortured publicly in the square in Merida. Thousands watched. All were silent. Red hot pincers tore open his flesh, making wounds in his abdomen, his hands, his feet, his knees, his head. Perhaps his intestines rolled from the wound at his side. Black blood poured from him. Iron bars broke all his bones. All this time he did not cry out. On his face was an expression of bliss and suffering. Did he enter into death peacefully? No one could tell from his expression at what moment he expired. At last his body was dismembered and cast upon the city refuse dump, where it was guarded until the flesh decomposed. *There are rains of little profit, rains from a rabbit sky, rains from a parched sky, rains from a woodpecker sky, high rains, rains from a vulture sky, crested rains, deer rains. There is fighting; there is a year of locusts. The diminished remainder of the population is hanged. They are defeated in war. Sad shall be the havoc at the crossroads.* Meanwhile, Garred Haus drives his Mercedes convertible down Santa Monica Boulevard. It is dark. Each car racing up and down the street weighs two or three tons: two or three tons enclosing mere pounds of flesh, of meat, of blood, of hair, fingernails, teeth, bones, intestines. Garred, one of these creatures, pulls his tons of metal and glass and rich upholstery to the curb. A boy gets in. Garred lifts an eyebrow: "How much?" "What do you want?" "Suck me off." "Give me twenty dollars." "While I drive, okay?" Garred opens his pants. *The kinkajou claws the back of the jaguar amid the affliction of the katun, amid the affliction of the year; they are greedy for domination.* Meanwhile, a line of horsemen descend the defoliated eastern slope of the hills, threading their way between ochre blossoms of napalm. Meanwhile, Osgood Fetters and Virginia White—breast tucked carefully into the bodice of her dress—stroll beneath the statue of the Virgin Mary, which is given pride of place high on the wall above them. Her bisque face shines. Her cheeks are plump and ruddy with health. Rich robes adorn her body. She looks down on the broken Jacinto Canek, or on her broken son Jesus, she looks down on the few wooden pews which remain on the ruined floor, on the rubble of brick and stone, and says nothing. *Then shall come to pass the shaking of the plumeria flower. Then you shall understand. Then it shall thunder from a dry sky. Then shall be spoken that which is written on the wall.* Meanwhile, Garred Haus, zipped back together, gives the boy $20 and some Big Mac coupons. The boy shuffles away, into the depths of Santa Monica Boulevard, wiping his mouth. Garred drives to a Denny's Restaurant. There are several in the city. The restaurant never closes. A hostess always greets you cheerfully. As Garred enters, an older couple are leaving. "Say," the man says, "arent you Gerald House, the actor?" "No." "He sure looks like Gerald House, dont he, ma?" "He surely does." "You sure you arent that feller?" "I'm sure." "I think Gerald House is younger," says the woman, "and he's got more hair." "Maybe youre right, ma." Garred goes in and says to the hostess, who is short and fat and has nothing to be cheerful about, "Give me a table in the back." She waddles towards the rear. "There's a meeting back here," she says, "is that all right?" "Just bring me coffee, okay?" Beyond him a man is speaking to a number of waitresses in their very gingham, very American, uniforms, plus one man in cook's whites. He is an *active* man, this speaker. He bobs up and down. He punctuates his words by slapping his fist into his hand. He continually smiles. "When they *finish* eating," he is telling his audience, "dont just walk up and *ask* if they want anything more. How do *they* know what they want? Do *they*

remember the menu? No, of course not. *Make* a suggestion. *Help* them
out. This month we're pushing strawberry pie. So go up to them and
say, How about a *nice* piece of *strawberry* pie. Youll be surprised how
many will say, Yeah, sure. But they *wont* say, Yeah, sure, unless you *tell*
them what they want—" "Shit," says Garred, loudly enough so the
nearest waitress, who has short brown hair and blank brown eyes, can
hear. He takes another sip of his coffee, leaves a dollar, and walks out
to his car. *"Son, bring me a very beautiful woman with a very white
countenance. I greatly desire her. I will cast down her skirt and her loose dress
before me." "It is well, father."* Meanwhile, the others have gathered in
the red room. When Garred returns they take their positions. The
woman removes her white dress. She lies on the burlap bed. The
iguana—the ppuppulni-huh—crawls toward her.

"I heard screams last night."

"Screams?"

"I'm certain of it."

"I heard nothing."

"I was awakened—they awakened me—"

"Awakened?"

"I dont know the time."

"You were possibly dreaming."

The priest lifts his head.

"No," he says. "I heard them, too."

"You?"

"Distinctly. Quite—quite distinctly—"

"Sound effects."

"What?" says the woman.

"Sound effects. If you heard anything at all."

They lie silent. After a while the woman begins to moan. The
ppuppulni-huh has crawled up between her legs. Its head is at the cleft
of her body. Oh, the woman says, oh, the woman moans, dont do that.
Oh, no, please, dont do that. The lizard sucks. Oh, no, oh no, the
woman moans, not that, oh please, not that. Her white body begins to
buck.

2

The day begins with everyone called to the set. Positions are allocated. The three actors are arranged on their burlap beds. It is early morning, or what is supposed to be early morning. One actor lifts a head: "Listen!" Another stirs: "I dont hear anything." The third: "It's a helicopter!" The three lines of dialogue are repeated. "Listen!" "I dont hear anything." "It's a helicopter!" The helicopter—a UH-1C— comes thump-thump-thumping over the hill, on cue. It looks like a flying black insect. Below it dangles a net filled with dark objects. The copter hovers a moment, and then releases one end of the net. Immediately the black objects fall. From this distance they look like bodies; perhaps they are merely papier-mâché heads and pants and shirts stuffed with kapok. "No, no ," an electronically amplified voice shouts, "you assholes, not in the trees!" The bodies have indeed fallen into the arms of a ceiba tree. Heads, legs, a few arms and torsos are caught in the branches. "Jesus Christ!" the voice roars. Even over the electronic amplification system the southern accent is distinguishable. "Jesus Christ! Cant you assholes do anything? Go on—get outa here! Get another load, and for Chrissake do it right!" Suitably chastened, head drooping, the insect-like helicopter thump-thump-thumps away over the hill. Petulantly it fires a couple of 2.5-inch rockets and a couple of bursts—at 6,000 rounds a minute—from its two XM-21 Miniguns. The trees below shake at the impact. Meanwhile, the horsemen, winding their way down the eastern hillside, pause to watch. A twin-engined UC-123 Provider passes overhead, a fine mist trailing behind it. The mist drifts through the ceiba trees, the red zapote, the tall balche trees, and onto the horsemen. They wipe the Dioxin from their faces, the 2,4,5-T from their hair. The ponies shake their heads. Then they continue. *The sea upon which I go burns. The face of the heavens is tilted.* Meanwhile, the woman Virginia White takes advantage of the break to stroll into the nearby mall. She wears her white dress. The bodice is askew—a white breast can be glimpsed rolling about. Around her waist is a red belt. On her feet are red shoes. Past her hurry people. Many of them appear bloated, like the bodies seen occasionally in the rice paddies. They have tiny, suspicious eyes. They are all very pale. They are going to Karen's Kloset ("Nothing over $10!") and Pay-Less Drugs and Sav-Mor Shoes. Virginia White stands in a line at Swiss Colony— which has nothing to do with the Swiss—near clear-plastic-wrapped boxes of homogenized cheese and wax-coated fruit. When her turn comes she asks a tall man for a cup of tea. "What kind?" "Just tea." "We've got Red Zinger, Purple Passion, Yellow Zinger, Spicy Tama-risk—" "No, no, just tea, regular tea." "Ma'am, we dont have regular tea. You want regular, we got regular coffee and decaf coffee—we got regular Coke and Diet Coke—" "Diet Coke." "Large, Extra Large, or Jumbo?" "Small." "Lady, our large is small." "Large, then. No ice. And warm it up." "Warm it up?" "Just put it in your microwave—just for a minute—" "Lady, we dont heat up Coke." "Just warm it—just a little." "Look, lady, I'll give it to you with no ice, if that's what you want. But we dont heat up Coke." "Just no ice, then." "Large, right?" "Small—yes, Large." He shakes his head and turns to his Coke machine. *There is knife-thrusting strife, purse-snatching strife, strife with the blowgun, strife by trampling people, stone-throwing strife. The fighting ends in the heart of the forest. There is sudden death with hunger; the vultures enter the houses because of pestilence.* Osgood Fetters, meanwhile, decides to bathe. He draws water up from the cenote. His naked body is lean, but fallen: that is, the muscles and the flesh seem slack. Within the water that he pours over himself, in the air around him, in the bat guano and the dirt and the limestone beneath his feet, are various organisms. There is the *Geoplana multipunctata*, with its hundreds of eyes, its sinuous ejaculatory duct , and its short female duct which enters the rear end of the atrium. There is the *Parabascoides yucatanensis* whose oral sucker is approximately the same size as its acetabulum, and the related *Anenterotrema auritum,* whose sperm ducts arise from the anteromedian ends of its testes. In the water are leeches, such as the *Glossihonia magnidiscus,* whose caudal sucker is a very large, thin disk, and whose anus is a conspicuous opening on the narrow caudal peduncle. In the dirt crawls an *Eodrilus oxkutzcabensis,* its copulatory pouches in front of its prostatic duct. Among the arachnida near Osgood's feet are the *Tarantula fuscimana, Schizomus cavernicolens,* the scorpion *Centrurus yucatanus,* whose ventral plates are shining but rugose, whose cauda are long and slender, whose keels are granular or subserrate, and the *Cryptocellus pearsei,* with its whitish carapace. The false scorpions abound, and include the *Pachychitra maya,* completely lacking eyes, but whose palps are robust, and the *Lustrochernes minor,* which possess eye spots but no true eyes, and the pallid *Parazaona cavicola.* Present also, unknown to Osgood Fetters, who is briskly drying himself, are the araneida and the nematodes, the acarinids and the cave crickets, the heteropterida and the ubiquitous blattida. In the bat feces are coleopterida, both larval and adult. Crawling every-where—they crawl over Osgood's feet—are the myrmicinae and the dolichoderinae and the formicinae. Some of these creatures may appear later, and will then be described in greater detail. Osgood, however, has finished bathing. He dresses: boxer shorts, loose slacks, socks and sandals, and a white shirt, which is left untucked. He returns to the red room, where, meanwhile, the woman Virginia White has returned also. *Then it was that fire descended, then the rope descended, then rocks and trees descended. Then came the beating of things with wood and stone. Then Oxlahun-ti-ku was seized, his head was wounded, his face was buffeted, he was spit upon, he was thrown on his back.* Meanwhile, the three actors are arranged once more on their burlap beds. Virginia White's hair is fluffed. More oily sweat is applied to Garred's face. Osgood's leg, still swollen, is propped up before him. One actor says: "Listen!" A second responds: "I dont hear anything." "No," says the third, "it's a helicopter!" The UH-1C comes thump-thump-thumping over the hill, on cue. The net, filled again, sways beneath it. "A little further!" booms an electronically amplified voice. "Keep coming. Keep coming. Keep—

all right, *now!*" One side of the net is loosened. Somehow, however—perhaps a gust of wind upsets it—the edge of the net catches on some protrusion beneath the helicopter. "Shit!" booms the voice. The net, with its grisly burden, real or not, swings from side to side, rocking the copter. The copter quickly descends, spitting fire from its exhausts. The rolling, swaying bodies in the net hit the ground. The landing wheels of the helicopter bounce on top of them. "Assholes!" booms the voice in undisguised electronic fury. "I dont think I can watch this," says Osgood Fetters. He limps out, past the cenote, past the bat guano, past the *Pachychitra maya*, which, lacking eyes, fails to see him, and then through the western or black room, into the garden. He passes the black laurel, the black ceiba tree of abundance, and the rows of black speckled corn. Black wild pigeons are flushed from the black tipped camotes. Black bees hum. Scent from the black Ix-laul fills the air. The air itself is blackened with clouds. At the end of the garden stands a white man. It is a moment before Osgood sees him. The man is soft, plump. His clothing bags around him. He is dressed in the green camouflage uniform of a soldier, perhaps a marine. His face is pallid, pellucid, although not blind: blue eyes have turned to look at Osgood. He is pissing. The penile organ itself, which he holds between the forefinger and thumb of his right hand, is pale and pellucid, perhaps hydrophylic, though lacking tactile or gustatory barbels. One might call him trogloxene, or perhaps euryphotic. Wisps of blond hair have escaped his duck-billed cap. He is pissing into the open mouth of a dead man. This dead man lies at the blackened end of the garden. His body is swollen; the skin taut. A trail of intestines leads from his stomach across the blackened grass. The boy who is pissing—he does not seem old enough to be a man—shakes his pellucid organ. A few golden drops of urine fly about. He tucks the organ away, bending slightly at the waist. He looks again at Osgood. "They told me to do it," he says. His words fly away in the wind. He begins to walk, limping a bit, like Osgood. *The face of the lord of the katun is covered; his face is dead. There is mourning for water; there is mourning for bread. His mat and his throne shall face the west. Blood-vomit is the charge of the katun.* Meanwhile, the horsemen have stopped at the edge of the forest. Five men are visible. They have dismounted. The details of their clothing and their armament are not clear at this distance. Meanwhile, Osgood, his face pale, has returned to the red room.

"There's a man out there—he was pissing—"

"Pissing?"

"On a dead man."

"Pissing on a dead man?"

"Pissing into his mouth."

"There's a man out there, you say—"

"A soldier, a marine—"

"What?" says Virginia White. "What are you saying?"

"There's a man out there—"

"Are you quite sure?" says Garred.

"I saw it—"

"You saw a man—a soldier—pissing into a dead man's mouth?"

"I saw it."

Garred gets up. He walks out. There is an embarrassed silence. Virginia White avoids looking at Osgood. One of her hands plucks at the torn cup of her brassiere. Then Garred returns. "There's nothing out there," he says. Osgood starts to protest. "Nothing," Garred says firmly. "Nothing at all."

3

The woman wears her white dress. Lights come on, illuminating her. Outside all is dark. Only the SP-2H Neptune cruises overhead. Occasionally—perhaps its Night Observation Scope or its Black Crow Truck Ignition Sensor has found a target—it lets loose a stream of tracer bullets or a load of incendiaries. When this happens everyone stops to watch. Conversation becomes general. People lean on each other to see out the windows. When the display is finished all resume their places. Garred's toupee is adjusted. Osgood's leg is placed just so. The white woman's bodice is arranged so more breast shows. A wardrobe woman sniffs: "No better than she needs to be, that one." The F-4 pilot next to her says: "I wouldnt mind a piece of that." The wardrobe woman nudges him with her elbow: "Coo, you men!" Angles are calculated. The actors begin to speak. "I'm going to complain." "We shall all complain." "This isnt a movie, it's a torture chamber." Occasionally they are interrupted. Lines are repeated with cameras at different positions. "I cant do my hair, I feel ugly." "No, no, everything will be all right, youll see." "I dont want to see." When the lights are turned off they make crackling noises as they cool. *The dog is its tidings; the vulture is its tidings. The opossum is its face to the rulers. Then came Hunpic-ti-ax as an affliction, the jaguar and Canul for an affliction. These were the eaters of their food, the destroyers of their crops, the boboch, the destroyer of food.* Meanwhile neither the artificial lights nor the flashing tracers have any effect upon the brotulid and synbranchid fish in the cenote. The brotulid, *Typhlias pearsei*, and the synbranchid, *Pluto infernalis*, are wholly devoid of eyes, even vestigial eyes. As the *Typhlias* swims in the black water its large, clasper-shaped penis emerges from the vulvate-like folds around it. The eel-shaped, *penile*-shaped *Pluto* emerges from a crevice: its head moves left and right as though searching for something it cannot, and never will, see. Meanwhile, the five horsemen have waited until dark to cross the open space. At last they tether their mounts to a ceiba tree. The lighting here is ochre and sporadic, supplied by the munitions of the Neptune, which continues to drone overhead. Because of the intermittent nature of the light these five men are indescribable until they enter the red room, where the gas lantern continues to hiss. This lantern casts a ruddy glow. The glow is so dim that special, ultra-sensitive film must be used to capture the following scene. Yet even so shadows shall predominate. Shadows shall exaggerate each movement. The camera position will be low— the figures thus looming and sinister—and the lens a wide angle, allowing both a deep focus and a certain distortion, a certain *disorientation*, of space. In this way is the first man illuminated in the doorway. He has a braid of red hair down the left side of his head. The right side of his head is shaved. He is lightly bearded. He, and the men who follow, are garbed in camouflage uniforms and festooned with weaponry: pistols, hand grenades, bandoliers, K-bars, dangling rifles. We identify two M-16s, one M-60, and an M-79 grenade launcher, among others. When the woman Virginia White sees the first man her face blanches. She has by now read several pages of her script, and recognizes what must necessarily follow. "No," she says, however, "*no*," she protests, "*wait*, I'm not ready." The man steps forward one pace. "Fucking *round* eye," he says. The second man is in the doorway, weapon erect. He is quickly followed by the third man. These two are both black and wear their hair in mohawks. One has long black hairs sprouting from his chin. The fourth man is white. The fifth man is white. He is plump, with pellucid cheeks. "Fucking *round* eye." "Let's dick her." "Fucking *A*, man." Her bodice is ripped wide. The one loose breast rolls. "Fucking *tits*, man." Osgood makes a feeble interventionary gesture. An M-16 fires six rounds—pop-pop-pop, pop-pop-pop. Stucco blasts from the wall. Osgood sits abruptly. "Fucking *tits*, man." The woman is thrown onto the floor. Her head bounces on the tile. She is stunned but conscious. "No, no—you cant—I'm not ready—" Her skirts fly up. "Fucking *cunt*, man." "Dick her." "Fucking *A*, man." She tries to squirm away. The black plastic stock of the Colt Armalite M-16 whacks the left side of her face. The sound is oddly hollow. The woman spits blood and what appears to be, in this dim light, white pieces of teeth. Her eyes are huge. "Fucking *still*, cunt." Her voice, when she speaks, will now be slurred. The words will be scarcely recognizable. We shall give careful attention to them. At all times a rifle barrel will be held close to her face, first an M-16, then the M-60, then the gaping muzzle of the M-79, which surely could not be used in such close quarters. The first man is already between her legs. His red ass rises and falls. Seconds later the next man is between her legs. His black ass rises and falls. "No, no, why are you doing this—" "Fucking *ass*, man." The third fucks her. While he fucks her, the fourth man grabs her by the ears. He lifts her face and turns it. He jams his pellucid but erect organ into her mouth. "Suck, bitch." Blood speckles the white shaft of this organ. "Fucking *suck*, bitch." The first man—he is identifiable, even in this dim, hissing light, by the red braid of his hair—is already back between her legs. The fifth man, however, is standing at her head. He has opened his pants and is fiddling with his dick. When the woman's head is thrown back down—it bounces again on the tile floor—this fifth man begins to piss on her. He holds his pale, perhaps hydrophylic organ between his thumb and forefinger. The woman sputters and gasps beneath this golden shower. The man between her legs is thumping her so hard she is being driven across the floor. All this is visible in the glow of the gas lantern, augmented occasionally by the ochre flare of incendiaries outside. All this, even where we have not specifically noted it, is deeply shadowed. It is not always clear what is happening, in spite of our careful review. The woman is driven—thump-thump-thump—across the tile floor, spitting blood, spitting semen, spitting urine, spitting teeth. Perhaps the darkness adds to the atmosphere of gloom and violence, or perhaps it is carefully planned to give an artistic dimension to the scene. Certainly the leaping shadows are dramatic. The low angle of the camera adds a special flair. Osgood's sorry face, his lugubrious face, is visible to one side. Garred's poise is feral, that is, like a wild animal prepared to leap. It is beyond his window that we see the Neptune SP-2H as tracers spit from its nose. It cruises the black night, spitting fire, illuminating the shadows and making the ground dance beneath it, as though the ground were itself celebrating its own death. *Then began their reign; then began their rule. Then they began to be served; then those who were to be thrown into the cenote arrived; then they began to throw them into the well that their prophecy might be heard by their rulers.* Meanwhile, the Neptune SP-2H has left the hills. Cries can now be heard. Rifles and RPGs and Swedish Ks open up, sending their tracers from the eastern hills to the western hills, and from the western hills to the eastern ones. All this, however, has no effect upon those in the building, where the rape scene is coming to an end. Each man seems sated. One has pissed as much as his bladder held, the others ejaculated until their testes ached. Their movements are now slower, turgid. The woman lies bloody on the floor. One man—the first one, the one with the red braid of hair—picks up his M-16 and injects the barrel into her vagina. "Fucking *A*, man." "Bust *caps*, man." He pulls the trigger. Fortunately for this book, and this film, the weapon fails to fire. The trigger clicks again and again. He jerks it from her cunt, tearing the tender flesh. "Fucking *carb*ine." He hurls it across the room, where it clatters against the wall. He takes the woman by her long hair and drags her across the floor. She leaves a trail of blood and semen from between her legs. The others herd Garred and Osgood. The building, of course, is shaped like a fat cross. The room they enter is in the center of the building. It is dark, except for the light from the lantern in the red room. Their shadows are thus thrown forward, to the edge of the cenote. The eight people gather at the edge of the cenote. They pause there for only a moment. "The fucking *water*, man." The woman is jerked by her hair half upright. Her hair looks particularly delicate in this dim light. Her dress is mostly off her body—held, in fact, only by her red belt. The one free breast rolls, and rolls. A boot shoves her. A little over a second later her body splashes into the water. Osgood and Garred follow, nudged forward by the barrels of, respectively, an M-60 and an M-16. The men then begin shooting into the cenote. The M-16 makes pop-pop-pop sounds. The

M-60 goes brrrrrp. A .45 automatic pistol makes the loudest noise of all. Smoke drifts in the air. Hot shell casings pile up around them. Finally one man—it is the one with the red braid—unhooks a grenade and tosses it into the cenote. The explosion it makes ends this scene. The sound reverberates away. After a moment there is an electronic squeal. Then:

"Fucking *round* eye."

"No, wait, I'm not ready."

"Fucking *tits*, man."

"Shee-*it*, man. Five times. And I'm a honkie, too."

"That's some Class-A organ, man."

"Let's dick her."

"No—you cant—I'm not ready—"

"With my old lady, I get it up once a week, man, I'm lucky."

"Fucking gun, man."

"Got that rapid fire *function*, man."

"No, no, why are you doing this—"

"Fucking *suck*, bitch."

"Get it on, honkie."

"Fucking *A*, man."

There is another high pitched electronic squeal. And then, finally, silence.

4

The woman is laid out on her burlap bed. Everyone gathers around
her. They inspect her wounds. Her labia are black with blood. Elsewhere she is bruised and torn. Her hair is a mat of reeds. Her cheeks
are swollen. They are like the swollen bisque cheeks of the Madonna.
Her eyes are brittle. They are like the brittle glass eyes of the
Madonna. Garred sticks a cigarette in his mouth. He rolls the pack into
the sleeve of his T-shirt. It was he, of course, who hauled the woman
from the cenote. He climbed out. The rope was lowered to Osgood,
who tied it under her arms. The black water luminesced around them.
She dripped water, like tiny lights, as Garred pulled her up the wall of
the cenote. She glowed, phosphorescent, sheeted with water. During
the night, they had all glowed. They had drifted under a high vaulted
ceiling of the two-cycle solution type cave. The current carried them.
Garred pulled himself onto a shelf of limestone. He helped Osgood,
and then, as she drifted near, the woman. Her dress had at last come
free from her body. It continued past, like a white soul loosed from its
flesh. The woman was garbed then only in the remains of her brassiere.
On the shelf of limestone they waited, perhaps for hours, perhaps all
night. They heard the bullets splat into the water of the cenote. They
heard the explosion of the grenade. Dead fish—silurids, brotulids, the
blind synbranchid *Pluto infernalis*—floated past. These fish were not
phosphorescent. They were dead. The walls, however, dripping water,
glowed, as though the walls were alive. *Their faces had been trampled on
the ground, and they had been overthrown by the unrestrained upstarts of the
day and of the katun, the son of evil and the offspring of the harlot, who were*

born when their day dawned in Katun 3 Ahau. Meanwhile, the Assistant Director enters with a syringe in his beefy hand. Meanwhile, the two F4s swoop low over the eastern hills, pummeling them. Meanwhile, Garred Haus wanders through the black garden. He has not stayed to watch the ministering to the white woman. He passes black flowers and black insects. He pauses at a row of five black heads. The heads are black with blood and their own decay. The heads are like turnips. They are lined up. Each has a cigarette in his mouth. The ears have been cut off. Doubtless someone, perhaps someone in the cavernous forest, the forest that has not been denuded by defoliants, is wearing the ears around his neck. Garred stares at the heads for only a moment. He grinds his own cigarette under his heel, leaving a charred mark in the dirt. He leaves. Meanwhile, the wardrobe woman has led the Neptune pilot to the wardrobe room. Hanging there are camouflage uniforms, white dresses, Ironweave Pantihose, boxer shorts, trousers, red belts, and delicate white brassieres, many with one cup torn loose. The wardrobe woman bares her ass. She does this by leaning forward and flipping her dress up onto her back. The Neptune pilot has sheathed his penis in black latex. He attacks her from behind. The woman grunts. The dresses sway. Uh-uh-uh-uh-uh, grunts the woman. The pilot gives a final lunge—a paroxysm of a lunge—and whoops. "Coo, you men," says the wardrobe woman as the black-sheathed penis withdraws. She pats her clothes into place. "Now dont you come out for a few minutes, hear? We dont want the others thinking anything, do we?" "Getcher ass in gear, then," says the pilot, grinning. The woman elbows him. "Coo!" *Then begins the lewdness of the wise men, the beckoning of the katun. The katun begins to limp; it is all over the world. Carnal sin is its garment, carnal sin is its face, carnal sin is its sandal, carnal sin is its head, carnal sin is its gait. They twist their necks, they twist their mouths, they wink the eye, they slaver at the mouth, at men, women, chiefs, justices, presiding officers, everybody both great and small. There is no great teaching. Heaven and earth are truly lost to them; they have lost all shame.* Meanwhile, Garred walks along the tracks. Old railroad cars stand there. The jungle is just beyond them. In places the jungle has reclaimed the railroad cars. Some of the railroad cars have words still visible on them: The Great

White Way. The Southern Route. Ferrocarilles de Sonora. Vive el Corean. Visible within one railroad car are three beefy men. They are playing cards and drinking tepid Cokes. They chew on cigars and Cheese Doritos. They glance at Garred as he passes. Below them, on the ground, men are working. They are slitting open the bellies of corpses. Using thickly gloved hands they pull the intestines into buckets. The buckets are carried away by boys. Into the abdominal cavities are placed packages wrapped in plastic. Another man—he is dressed in white—sews the abdomens back together. The bodies are then put into heavy rubber bags and lifted into another railroad car. The intestines are yellow, red, and black, and emerge in great looping coils. Because of the stench everyone wears gauze masks. Garred does not. He hurries past, past men holding Uzis and MAC-10s, past men holding clipboards, past diesel trucks, filled with black rubber bags, past spitting children, past Congressmen with sweaty faces and rotund bellies, past a steam engine hissing on rusty tracks, past railroad cars filled with whores, past cages holding prisoners of both sexes and several races, past cook shacks where T-bones are frying, past piles of rags that women are picking through, past graves marked with sticks, crosses, and plumeria flowers, past piles of ears, some of them plastic, past briefing rooms, past pilots with "Air America" tattooed on their biceps, past marines sleeping in the shade of ceiba trees, past television reporters in safari shirts, past wrecked helicopters and APCs and Caribous and six-bys and T-54s sagging on their treads. Finally he pauses at the last row of railroad cars. "Hey, GI! You want fuckee-suckee?" Women whistle and lift their sarongs, their saris, their skirts, their legs, their asses, their breasts. Garred goes up to one. A small boy lies with his face in her lap. The woman has dark, thin lips. Her eyes shine like polished copper. "GI got dollar?" "I got dollar." "You want fuckee-fuckee?" "I want fuckee-fuckee." "You give me five dollar." Garred taps the boy's rump. "I want fuckee-fuckee boy." For a moment the woman says nothing. The boy does not stir. "You give me ten dollar." She holds out her hand. When Garred finishes, the little boy is crying. The woman watches Garred walk away. Then she turns to the boy and slaps him. *Then descended Bolon Mayel, the fragrant one;*

sweet was his mouth and the tip of his tongue. Sweet were his brains. Then descended the two mighty demon bats who sucked the honey of the flowers. Then there grew up for it the red unfolded calyx, the white unfolded calyx, the black unfolded calyx, the yellow unfolded calyx. Then there sprang up the five-leafed flower, the five drooping petals, the ix-chabil-tok, the little flower, ix macuil xuchit, the flower with the brightly colored tip, the laurel flower, and the limping flower. Meanwhile the red room is quiet. The lantern hisses. Shadows gather in the corners. The white woman's swollen face turns right and left. Osgood sits at her side. His shadow is cast onto the wall. Garred sits on his bed. His shadow is cast onto the wall. After a while the woman tries to speak. She tries to speak through her bruised and broken mouth. Osgood leans forward. "What? What? I dont think you should talk." "I saw something." "You saw something?" The pupils of her eyes are dilated. They wander right and left. Garred, unlit cigarette dangling from his lips, comes to the woman's bed.

"What did you see?"

"The cenote is a mirror."

She breathes heavily for a moment.

"I saw it," she says.

"You saw—the cenote—as a mirror?"

"It is a mirror."

"Anything else?"

"I saw people below."

"People?"

"When I tried to look at them they beat me."

"I see."

"They called me Ix Zacbeliz."

"What does that mean?"

"I dont know."

She breathes heavily again. Her eyes wander up and down, right and left. She is silent. She does not speak. Only her breath can be heard. At last the hissing lantern is quiet. The shadows move freely through the room. The Ix Zacbeliz—the white woman who travels on foot—lies on her burlap bed. Her flower is agape. Red mucencabs—the wild bees who drink honey from flowers—cluster around it. Her white and red blossom is their cup. Then come the black mucencabs. Then come the yellow mucencabs. Then come the white mucencabs. They drink from her. Then comes Nohyumcab, the lord of the hive. Her blossom is his cup. Then come the black bats. They drink from her. Then comes Ah Puch, scepter in hand. His red eyes glow. Her blossom is his cup. Then comes Hapay Can, the sucking snake. He drinks from her. Her blossom is his cup. They cluster at her open flower, at her five petaled flower, at her five unfolded calyx. Then comes the ppuppulni-huh. He crawls up to her. His tongue flicks, once, twice. He lays his throat, his soft throat, on her wounded flower.

The day begins as scheduled. Positions are taken as directed. A fleshy boy in jungle fatigues jiggles his dick. "There's a man out there." "Are you quite sure?" "I saw him." Men and women with coppery eyes press their faces at the windows. The white woman puts on her red high-heeled shoes. "I need a break." She walks to the nearby mall. Meanwhile, stubby A-1 Skyraiders, capable of carrying 8,000 pounds of external ordnance, and Vought A-7 Corsair IIs, single seat jet attack planes, begin appearing overhead. They circle along with Caribou C-7s, a few Republic F-105 Thunderchiefs armed with 20mm Gatling guns, and one AC-47 Dragonship. Mingling with the airplanes are CH47s, some loaded with up to 65 troops, and Sikorsky H34 Choctaws. The SP-2H Neptune, with its FLIR and LLLTV Sensors blinking and flickering, is joined by an Aeronavale PB4Y Privateer. Soon others will appear. As they appear we shall describe them. All of them circle overhead, waiting their cue. *There shall come multitudes who gather stone and wood, the worthless rabble of the town. Fire shall flame up at the tips of their hands. Prepare yourselves to endure the burden of misery which is to come among your villages.* Meanwhile, in the mall everything is ready. The people are arranged. They stand at intervals in front of the shops. Every fourth person is obese. Some have tiny eyes. These eyes are sullen. The eyes do not move. The eyes glower: tiny, sullen, staring straight ahead. When the white woman passes in front of them, the eyes do not acknowledge her presence. The white woman wears her red shoes with very high heels. She wears her white bra with its one cup torn away. Her face is swollen, like the swollen bisque face of the

Madonna. Her eyes are brittle, like the brittle glass eyes of the Madonna. Her flower is crusted with black blood. Young girls hiss at her. These young girls stand in front of boutiques. Each boutique has a name like Hot Metal, or Deep Pink. The young girls stand in small groups. They hiss as the white woman passes. They hiss as the white woman walks by. The woman goes to Swiss Colony. She stands in line. When her turn comes she tells the tall man she wants tea. "Red Zinger, Purple Zinger, Orange Zinger—" "No, Diet Coke." "Large, Extra Large, Jumbo—" "Small—I mean, Large. And heat it up." "Lady, we dont heat Coke." "Just a little—" "Lady, we dont heat Coke." "No ice, then." There is a *Holocompsa zapoteca* climbing the wall. The woman plucks it from the wall. She bites off its head. She puts the rest of it in her mouth. "Lady, that's disgusting." "It's *your* cockroach." "I'm calling the security guards." The five security guards come. They jostle her. They tug at her arms, they pluck at her mat of hair. Their hands anonymously brush her buttocks, squeeze her breasts, stroke her belly. They put her down on the floor. They pry open her mouth and take out the remains of the *Holocompsa zapoteca*. One of the guards puts his hand between her legs. Fingers grope at her. Then they escort her to the door. "Dont come back," they warn. She steps out across the acres of hot asphalt. Cars race by. Overhead pass a squadron of B-57s and a lone F-100 Supersabre from the 429th Tactical Fighter Squadron. Douglas A-26 Invaders thunder past. Following more slowly are UH-1Cs, UH-1Ds, UH-1Hs, UH-1Ls, and a few UH-1Ms, their blades making thump-thump-thump sounds. Even slower is the Antonov AN-2, a fabric-covered, single-engined biplane with a wooden scimitar propeller. The pilot looks down and waves, or perhaps makes a threatening gesture. *Then it shall shake heaven and earth. In sorrow shall end the katun of the plumeria flower. No one shall fulfill his promises. The prop-roots of the trees shall be bent over. There shall be an earthquake all over the land.* Meanwhile, the woman continues walking. Night appears to have fallen. This, however, may be a trick. A filter may have been placed over the lens of the giant Panavision camera. If that is so, the moon which appears to be high in the sky is actually the sun, filtered. Nevertheless all is coordinated. The cars as they race past have their headlights on. The street lamps appear to glow. The woman walks, in her red high-heels, past boys and girls who stand patiently on the street corners, dimly lit. One of them is the boy Garred picked up not long ago. The boy appears very sweet. The camera examines him. Then he turns his face. A sly smile appears. A white fluid begins to dribble from the corners of his mouth. Quickly we move away. The woman continues past open doorways. Through these doorways may be glimpsed stairways, some rising, some descending. An occasional balam stands there, or a kinkajou, or a Quetzal bird with iridescent feathers. Sometimes men stand at the tops of stairs. Sometimes women stand at the bottoms of stairs, wearing masks. The white woman does not pause. Meanwhile, a T-28 hurtles past, followed by a U-17 and a Volpar and a pair of Pilatus Porters. Joining them are Douglas SDB Dauntless dive bombers, a single F6F Hellcat, and a SB2C Helldiver. Easily identifiable, lumbering low over the hills, is a PBY-5A Catalina and a Grumman JRF Goose. Meanwhile, the woman passes an alley. Standing there, half obscured by the darkness, is a boy in camouflage uniform. A rifle is slung by its strap over one shoulder. The boy's face is pale, pellucid, wet with sweat. He is pissing. His organ is held between his thumb and forefinger. It is not clear what he is pissing on, or into. The boy shakes his dick and tucks it away. He watches the woman in red high-heels pass. He says nothing, but he does move his lips, licking them. At last the woman returns to the cross-shaped building, where the crew have been practicing tai chi and tae kwon do. She arrives at the same time as the O-1, the O-2, the OV-10A Black Ponies, the A-4 Skyhawks, some carrying 2,000 pound bombs, the F-8 Crusaders, who are not on a crusade, the UC-123 Providers, who provide a fine trailing mist of Dioxin, the C-47s laden with their electronic gear, the RF-4s providing reconnaissance, the T-33 Shooting Stars—they shoot across the black sky—and finally, the F4U Corsairs. The woman takes her place. Lights hiss as they turn on. Makeup people circulate, touching up the sweaty faces. Garred's toupee is adjusted. Osgood's leg is placed just so. "Listen," says one of them, perhaps Osgood. "I dont hear anything," another replies. "No," says the third, "it's a helicopter." The helicopters swoop in. Each copter dangles a net. The first copter is an

HH-3E. Bodies plummet from its net to the ground. It is followed by an H-21C. Its bodies plummet to the ground. Then comes an H-46 Sea Knight. Its bodies plummet to the ground. Then comes the CH-3C, and the Cobras, the CH-47s, the Sikorsky H-34s, and a line of UH-1s— the UH-1C, the UH-1D, the UH-1H, the UH-1L, and finally the UH-1M. Each releases its net of blackened bodies which plummet to the ground. An electronic voice shouts: "Yes! *Now!*—Yes! *Now!*—Yes! *Now!*" Heads roll over the ground. Torsos bounce right, torsos bounce left. It is difficult for us to identify the ages, sexes, races, and nationalities of these torsos, these heads, these arms, these legs. All of them bounce, roll, break apart. Finally the last helicopter thump-thump-thumps into the distance. "Fucking *A!*" cries the electronic voice. *Their hearts are submerged in sin. Their hearts are dead in their carnal sins. They sit crookedly on their thrones; crookedly in carnal sin. They are the unrestrained lewd ones of the day, the unrestrained lewd ones of the night, the rogues of the world. They twist their necks, they wink their eyes, they slaver at the mouth, at the rulers of the land, lord. Behold, when they come, there is no truth in the words of the foreigners to the land.* Meanwhile, the blackened and denuded hills are silent. The black sky is silent. The helicopters have fled, except for one, an H-23 loaded with cameras. All wait. Sweat drips from faces. The ppuppulni-huh crawls into the white woman's arms. The wardrobe woman rearranges her skirt. Key grips, sound men, gaffers crouch at the windows. Then the first jet makes its bombing run. It comes out of the west. It comes low over the building. The sound is like thunder from a dry sky. It unloads its napalm on the eastern hills. The jet shrieks away. It is followed, however. It is followed by another F-4, and then the A-1s, the A-7s, the C-7s, the F-105s. These are followed by gunships, spraying six thousand rounds a minute. The eastern hills shake. The black stumps of trees collapse. Cameras catch all of it. There are cameras in the H-23. There are cameras on the open ground. There are cameras mounted on platforms on the dome of the cross-shaped building . There are mobile cameras and stationary cameras. Men race through the gardens, carrying cameras. Other electronic instruments capture sounds. Each roar, each shriek, each peal of thunder is captured on electronic tape. They capture the sounds of the

Dauntless dive bombers and the Pilatus Porters and the T-28s, the Volpar and the Antonov and the Supersabre, the Shooting Stars and the Privateers, the Goose and the Catalina, the Marlin and the Orion, the Hellcats and the Helldivers. Electronic voices shriek in glee. "Keep coming! Keep coming! Fucking A!" Finally the B-52s—so high overhead they are scarsely visible—begin dropping their ordnance. They drop 500 pound bombs, and 750 pound bombs. They drop 1,000 pound bombs, and 2,000 pound bombs. They do this in conjunction with ordnance fired from PT-76 tanks, 80,000 pound tanks, Sheridan tanks and Patton tanks. APCs fire M-60s. 122mm rockets flash past. 60mm mortars fire, and 57mm guns, and Hawk surface-to-air missiles, and 155mm howitzers, and 104mm howitzers, and 175mm artillery, and five-inch shells from ships offshore. There are Walleyes and Willy Petes exploding, and napalm, and tear gas, and Bouncing Bettys, and CBUs. M-14s mounted with Starlight infra-red night sights begin to fire, along with M-16s and Kalashnikovs and Uzis and MAC-10s and Swedish Ks and Stoner 63s and CAR-15s. Ochre tracers flash across the arch of the sky. All this is caught on film and on tape. One camera focuses on the explosions caused by 1,000 pound bombs dropped from a B-52. These explosions move slowly along the eastern hills. They follow in a line, one after another. The explosions are like flowers that burst open. Their calyx unfold. Their petals unfold. The earth bursts into the air like flowers bursting open. Each step is visible. The 1,000 pound bombs continue across the open space. One falls into the eastern, or red garden, onto the red zapote and the red ceiba. One bomb falls onto the red room itself, another onto the dome which is set, as we have said, in the belly of the cross-shaped building. One bomb falls into the black room. A final bomb falls into the black garden, dispersing the five black heads, which look like turnips, the black-speckled corn, the black mucencabs, the black laurel, the pupae hanging from the black ceiba tree, the plumeria, the white, the red, the scarlet plumeria, and the balam, whose fur is thick with oil. When this happens the filter is removed from the last camera. It is daylight, as we have suspected. Small fires glow on the eastern hills. Smoke rises into the bright air, the air blazing with sunlight. The sky is empty. The earth is littered with craters, with metal, with bricks, with concrete. The cross-shaped building is mostly rubble. The dome has collapsed. The cenote is visible. The air is so bright that we have to blink our eyes. What a change, from night to day! We move away from the rubble, from the steaming earth, the blackened earth. After a moment I stop and turn around.

"What are you staring at?"

"Nothing."

"Nothing?"

"Nothing at all."

"Let's go, then."

She takes my arm. We leave.

PART FOUR

1

The first draft of this novel I wrote during five months wandering through Mexico. I mention this because it may be important for an understanding of this book. I have been a wanderer all my life. My life has been episodic, scattered around the world. It is not a life one would choose. I am a stranger everywhere I go. Nevertheless I am alive, which is perhaps a victory of sorts. Three fortune tellers predicted I would not survive into middle age. One was a Chinese in Decker Street, in Singapore. Another—long ago—was a Parsi woman in Bombay. My future embarrassed and flustered her. The last was a self-proclaimed psychic in Yucaipa, California, surely an exotic place. Yet I see today that my beard is gray, and that my hair is becoming gray. It is not a young man that peers from my mirror. I am middle-aged, and I am alive. I ascribe my survival to my constant wandering. Death could never catch up to me. It is amusing, at least, to think this. It is as good an explanation for my life as any. I have been fleeing death. During the course of this novel I fled death in Lagos de Moreno and Merida, in Aguascalientes and Uruapan. I hid in Guanajuato, in the Casa Kloster. I moved quickly through Querétero and Morelia. I slipped into Xalapa. I write this now in Pátzcuaro. I am in the Hotel Valmen. The sun enters from my right, through a tall window. Birds sing in a courtyard to my left. Altogether it is a pleasant enough place. The town itself is quiet. Tourists come here for the Indian market and to see Janitzio, a town on an island in the nearby lake. It is amusing to watch the tourists and guess where they are from. The Americans are the easiest. Many of them dress as Indians. They go into the mercado and buy white pants or cotton skirts. They put on sandals and straw hats. The women wrap shawls around their shoulders. We saw one of these Americans this morning. We were crossing the plaza chica. We were on our way to breakfast. The woman was middle-aged herself. She had a pale face with a silly smile on it. She seemed pleased with herself.

"Americans," I said, "are a costumed people."

"Costumed?"

"They have so little identity of their own they must constantly put on costumes, and pretend to be something they are not. But the disguise is always superficial, like their television."

"She seems happy."

"She seems silly."

"Perhaps Americans are only happy when they are silly."

"She reminds me," I said, "of Virginia White."

"Is that what happens to her? She becomes a middleaged 'Indian' in Pátzcuaro?"

"No. But that is an idea."

An episodic life produces an episodic novel, that is what I am trying to say. This novel appeared piece by piece. When I become too comfortable in any one place I moved on. The novel, like the life, is thus oddly discontinuous. It is discontinuous, episodic, segmented. This continues to be true even now, in Pátzcuaro, as I write these final pieces.

We came to Pátzcuaro to see the film of *Maya*. It has never been released in the United States. Doubtless this is because the film is so terrible. Perhaps someday it will appear on late night television or videocassettes. In the meantime the countries of the third world will absorb virtually any film, no matter how badly done, that has a blonde American actress in it. Virginia White, therefore, may be considered responsible for this movie's appearance in Mexico. Photographs of her are prominently displayed on the posters outside the theatre. Her bare breasts, unfortunately, have been inked out. This is a common practice in Mexico. In relatively sophisticated places like Mexico City and Guadalajara, where these movies first appear, the posters remain unmarked. As films progress through the countryside, which is more conservative, exhibitors begin inking over breasts and buttocks. Sometimes they draw brassieres and slips and panties on the bare flesh. There is something titillating about all these women blacked out with ink. I have wondered at times if the exhibitors do this to make the films seem more salacious than they actually are. No one, however, blacks out scenes of violence. In the posters of the film playing with *Maya* can be seen stakes driven through foreheads, blood bursting from bodies riddled by machine guns, and so on. Violence is clearly more acceptable than nude women. A naked breast, we may assume, is more dangerous than an M-60. No one goes so far as to ban these films, however, no matter how titillating they may be. They are the mainstay of the Mexican cinemas. Men will line up for hours to see them, especially on Sundays. The theatres fill with restless men, shuffling their boots, spitting on the floor. They pay the equivalent of about fifty cents to see someone like Virginia White bare her breasts. This seems a bargain. I would pay fifty cents any time to see Virginia White's breasts moving on a picture screen. No one could complain about their size, shape, or the profound delicacy of their nipples. It is unfortunate that the woman never learned to act. Whenever she is on the screen, you can see that she is yearning to turn to the camera and smile. That is all she really wants to do. She seems a little embarrassed at having to bare her tits so often, but it is all for the sake of art, isnt it? Besides, she is proud of her tits. One can see, throughout the film, this conflict running through her. She wishes to show off her tits. She wishes to demurely hide them. She is proud of them. She is embarrassed by them. But even in the middle of her embarrassment, as her face flushes, she yearns to turn to the camera and smile.

The movie, of course, has been retitled for its Mexican release. It is now called *El Sacrificio Sexual de las Mayas*. The ambiguity of this title is interesting. We discussed it this morning, after breakfast. We were walking through the cemetery which starts just beyond the mercado. I like Mexican cemeteries with their encrypted bodies, their anarchic jumble. No two tombs are alike. Sarcophagi, some broken, are everywhere. Stelae are moss-covered. We stopped at a large englassed crypt. Within were perfect plastic flowers and a large, gaudy picture of the Virgin Mary.

"I think you're wrong about the Mexicans," she said to me.

"In what way?"

"I think they prefer the Virgin Mary to Virginia White."

"The men, you mean?"

"The women, too."

It is certainly true that the Virgin Mother—resplendent, glowing—is given prominence in Mexican churches. Jesus, on or off his cross, will be relegated to a side chapel. Often we saw women crawling across the floor, kissing the tile at each pause. Others walked on their knees, gazing raptly at the indifferent, serene face high above. But one seldom saw men adopt these attitudes of reverence. I pointed this out.

"No, they dont need to. They *marry* the Virgin."

"Ah. Their wives—"

"Precisely. Who then play the role as perfectly as they can. Have you seen how Mexican women adore their male children?"

"The spoiled brats."

"The Virgin Mother holding the infant Jesus—that's what the Mexican women copy. They adore their sons, and mostly ignore their daughters."

"Yes, I've noticed."

"I didnt know you were so fond of tits."

"What?"

"You were going on there about Virginia White's bosom, werent you?"

"Well, just for the sake of illustration—"

"A bit tiresome, this masculine obsession with tits."

"I assure you—"

"Yes. Youre a leg man, arent you? Or so you say."

It is never wise to continue conversations like this with a woman. I mentioned the Spanish title of the film. Had she noticed the ambiguity in the wording? She nodded.

"But I doubt if it was on purpose," she said. "I think they just wanted the words 'sex' and 'sacrifice' in the title somewhere."

"The Mayas did sacrifice women—presumably virgins."

"Presumably."

"Or does the title suggest," I said, "that the Mayas themselves were sacrificed, sexually? I mean one could argue—"

"And doubtless you will."

"One could argue—couldnt one—that the Spanish invasion of Yucatan was a kind of rape."

"Quite literally, when it came to the native women."

"But *symbolically*. The army of men—those lances, and spears, the muskets—the horses—"

"I do rather like the horses."

"And didnt the Kaiser—I mean, during World War I—didnt the Germans keep referring to their country in masculine terms, as in the Fatherland—and the Low Countries and France, which they invaded, in feminine terms?"

"What are you trying to make of this?"

"And the American invasion of Vietnam—it was an invasion, wasnt it?—those tanks, the artillery—"

"Youre not only obsessed with tits, youre obsessed with symbolism, arent you?"

I shut up. We walked silently through the graves. After a moment she knelt at a small mound of dirt and a wooden cross. On the cross was the name Paco Garcia, handwritten in black paint. It was easily the smallest, least opulent grave in the area. A little farther along I could see a field of corn, and then rows of adobe houses. The sky was black towards the west, but here we could feel the sun on our shoulders.

"Poor little Paco," she said.

She stood up and looked at all the marble and stonework and glassed-in cages of the dead around us.

"I'll bet," she said, "I'll bet he was loved more—more than all these—"

She gestured, head thrown back. Her eyes were suddenly fierce.

"You may be right," I said.

"I am right."

She stalked off. I followed.

3

Pátzcuaro is famous for its market. It is divided into sections. At one place Indians sit at long wooden tables with their fish. These are black bass and carp and live axolotls, which look like big tadpoles, and of course the prized pescado blanco. But there are fewer of these fish, in particular the white fish, every year. The lake from whence they come is gradually turning into a swamp. It is fed by runoff from the hills. But the hills have been largely deforested. Silt washes down each year into the lake, which was already shallow. Water lilies and hyacinths are choking the waterways. Sewage descends with the silt, washing down with blood from the slaughterhouse. This is not, of course, a problem for me. I am only a visitor. It is a problem for the Mexicans, in particular the Indians who live off the lake. These Indians are called Purépecha. They once had a civilization which rivaled that of the Aztecs. Their capital, named Tzintzuntzan, lies now in ruins. Tourists visit it. It is only a few miles from Pátzcuaro. Everything dies, of course. Old civilizations. Cities. Races and cultures. People and lakes. One cannot dwell on such things, or on the accumulation of misery, the weight of eons of suffering. Yet death is visible everywhere. It is even visible in the market. We walked through it after the cemetery. At first glance all was the bustle of life. People gathered there from the neighboring villages. The market was bursting with produce, with fruit and meat, with cheese and bread, the wealth of the earth. There had been a rain earlier, and the ground was wet. We walked over cantaloupe skins and crushed tomatoes, peppers ground into asphalt. Bananas, including the huge ostions and the tiny dominicos, lay everywhere, turning black.

Papayas, plucked from their trees, were already dead. Rot had settled in everywhere. Apples had wormholes and brown spots. Carrots were limp. The Indians, the remnants of the dying Purépecha, stared at us with coppery eyes. We stopped at a display of pig heads. Their snouts were soft to the touch, very pale and delicate, and very dead. But there was noise everywhere, the noise of life, amid the dying grapes and ciruelos, the hanging slabs of beef and pork, the salchichas, the flesh ground up into sausages, the chorizo that we ate daily between soft tortillas, sustaining ourselves. We passed great round slabs of cheese. We smiled at the Indian women presiding over their baskets of bread. We passed tables laden with dead food, supplied by the earth, the earth that was washing down into the lake below, killing it.

We stopped at La Princesa Restaurant to sip at tepid Cokes.

"All this," I said, gesturing at the scene before us, "this mixture of death and life—does it ever bother you? Do you ever get depressed, watching it? Or angry?"

"Never."

"Why not?"

"Why not? Why on earth should I?"

"It depresses me."

"You must remember I am a woman."

"I wont forget *that.*"

She silenced me with a look.

"Dont be cute," she said. "It doesnt suit you."

"Well, go on, then."

"I am a woman. I am capable of creating life. And when I dont create life, every month I discharge blood from my body. I am—involved— in all this."

"This market—"

"You like symbols. This market is me. All this life, and this death— this ripeness, this decay—that is what I am. That is what a woman is."

"I'm not sure—"

"You are a man. You make a good beast of burden, carrying fruit to the market. And youre good at sowing, too, at planting, I'll admit that. But the fruit itself—all this produce—the market—the earth—all of that is female. That is why I sometimes despise you men."

"Despise us?"

"Because of what you do to the earth. You are cruel. If you had your way, you would destroy everything."

"I dont think I am cruel."

"Arent you? But in any case we are talking in generalities, arent we? About men—not a man. About women."

"Women are cruel too."

"Yes, we are cruel. I can be cruel. I was cruel the other night. I bit you."

I winced.

"Yes," I said. "The mark is still there."

"That was no love bite. I was angry."

"Why?"

"At your failure to acknowledge me."

"I dont understand."

"That's what I mean."

We sipped at our Cokes. They were cloying with sugar.

"Let's talk about something else," I said.

"All right. I notice you are limping again. Your ankle?"

"Yes. I stepped on a loose rock at the cemetery."

I had sprained the ankle a month earlier, in Aguascalientes, playing baseball with Gallo and his relatives. It was still weak and inflamed.

"It's nothing," I added.

"I noticed Osgood Fetters was limping all through the film."

"Like me, you mean?"

"He is your character."

"I think I look more like Garred. We're both blond—"

"Your belly is flatter."

"Yes, there is that."

"What happened to them? After the movie, I mean. They didnt die in that explosion, did they?"

"No, no. That was all special effects. No, Osgood went back to New York. He has a rent-controlled apartment there, you know."

"I thought he was adequate in the film."

"Yes. Competent. Nothing more, I'm afraid. Well, it was his first and last movie, anyway. He still acts once in a while on stage—community theatre, that kind of thing. And works for his lawyers."

"Is he writing?"

"No. Once in a while he talks about it. But no—just briefs, letters, case notes. He's getting old, you know. He looks bonier and bonier all the time. But he isnt as bitter as one might expect. He really thought he was good, you see. As a writer, I mean. And to never be acknowledged—well, that would make anyone bitter. But he seems to find a kind of—oh, odd pleasure—in his bitterness. He enjoys it. You know what I mean? His bitterness animates him, you see, and this animation—this pleasure—keeps the bitterness from being—from being—"

"Too bitter?"

"Exactly."

"So he is reasonably content?"

"Who knows? He's a solitary fellow. But at least he isnt consumed with anger."

"And Garred?"

"Ah, yes. Garred. That's another story. Look, shall we go on? I cant take any more of this Coke. How about a *feminine* taco in this *female* market?"

"You are a sweet man," she said.

Perhaps she meant it. She took my arm as we started across the market.

4

Pátzcuaro is an old town, a 16th century town. It lies in the hills of Michoacán. It is chilly at night. The morning sun, however, comes through the window, warming me as I sit at my typewriter. From the window I can see adobe walls marching up the hillside to the basilica, which I can glimpse just beyond some trees. The red tile roofs are all blackened with age. The streets below are paved with flat stones. At the corner, sitting near the entrance to Muebles San Jose ("Lo que su hogar necesita nosotros lo tenemos!"), is an old man with a wooden cart, selling ciruelos and peanuts. A policeman stands at the intersection periodically blowing his whistle, though at what is not clear. Earlier today school children marched down to the plaza chica, or the Plaza Gertruda Bocanegra, as it is properly called, after a local heroine of the Revolution. The children marched quite in step. They blew bugles and beat at drums. Speeches were made in the plaza. Then a marathon began, the runners leaving from Parroquia El Santuario, trotting along behind police cars with sirens wailing. Later in the day there will be a parade. It will pass beneath the hotel, skirt the plaza, and end at the Parroquia. All this is in celebration of Columbus' discovery of the Americas, the discovery which made the invasions of Cortez and Pizzaro and Francisco de Montoya possible. What was interesting to me, however, was the sense of community displayed. The school children in their uniforms, the men and women lining the streets—all of them belonged here. All of them, that is, except the Indians, who came into town from their villages and stayed close to the market, and the people like me, too tall, too red, too foreign to blend in. I was as much a stranger here as I was in the streets of southern California. Or Kudat, in Borneo. Or Darwin, or Mombasa, or Tangier. I suppose that was why I liked Garred. He too was an outsider, and knew it.

"But so was Osgood."

"Yes. But Osgood never accepted it. He wanted to belong. It was part of his despair, part of his bitterness, that he could never fit in."

"And Garred didnt mind?"

"Garred made it part of his life. He became a *dangerous* man."

"Dangerous?"

"Like an old elephant outside the herd. Short tempered, rather vicious. Unpredictable. And rather proud of his alienation."

"I will never forgive what he did to that boy."

"And to Virginia?"

"Given the context, I am more irritated with her. I despise the games such women play."

"Yes, you would."

We were in the Restaurant Los Escudos, on the plaza grande, having coffee. The tables were covered with cloth. The waiter wore a white jacket. We couldnt often afford to eat there, but we could drink their coffee. Outside, the marathoners passed for the second time, behind the wailing police car. Now there was a group of four in the lead, the rest straggling behind. School children, released from their duties but still in uniform, cheered them on. Bringing up the rear, far behind, were two fat men, flesh bouncing, faces bursting, soggy already with sweat. The school children jeered.

Pátzcuaro is unusual in having two plazas. The plaza chica I think of as the Indian plaza. The market begins there. The hotels around it are poor, run down. The plaza is busy, noisy, dirty, full of the swarthy Purépecha. The second, larger one is named after Don Vasco de Quiroga, a Spanish bishop sent from Spain in response to complaints by the Indians of maltreatment. This plaza is quiet. Around it one finds the expensive hotels and restaurants, like Los Escudos. Children play in the grass, and pretty women stroll about, arm in arm, in the evenings. It is a peaceful place, and we often go there in the afternoon to sit and read. If it begins to rain—we are at the end of the summer rainy season—we hurry into Los Escudos for coffee. On this day clouds piled up to the west, but the rain still held off.

Because of the two plazas, Pátzcuaro seems divided in half, as is much of Mexico: the poor and the rich. The villagers and the townspeople. The Indians and the mestizos. But in the towns like Pátzcuaro and the provincial cities like Aguascalientes, the culture somehow holds together. Only in Mexico City, and perhaps now Guadalajara—with their urban poor, the crime, the palpable misery, the poisonous air—does the center fail to hold. In this respect Mexico City is like an American city, or one of the old English manufacturing centers like Manchester. One sees there the despair of modern, Western life, the spiritual failure of a civilization. Osgood would rail against it. Garred would move through it, through the underworld, in this case more like a panther than an elephant, sleek, vicious, burning, his ochre eyes triumphant.

"Is that where he is now? In New York, or Hamburg?"

"No, no. Although he did go back to Europe, where he made a couple more films."

"And is he European? German?"

"He never liked to say. He liked being—secretive. But he spoke several languages, including German, quite fluently."

"You speak of him in the past tense."

"You noticed."

"So he died?"

"He died."

"Let me guess. He contracted AIDS."

"Youre too quick for me."

"You are so obvious."

"Well, why not? It is such a modern disease—and such an American one."

"Yet it began—"

"I know, I know. In Africa, where it has been even more devastating. But I think of it as an American disease—or as a modern, Western, Christian disease. Americans are so righteous about it, so judgmental—"

"Yes, yes, we know your thoughts on the subject. But Garred—how did he take it? Did he suffer?"

"Do you want him to have suffered?"

The tip of her tongue appeared between her teeth as she thought. "Yes," she finally said. "Why not? He would suffer anyway, and probably find pleasure in it."

"Youre right. As the symptoms appeared—the lesions, the emaciation—-he seemed to gloat. As though the pain, the corruption, proved something. And of course he spread the disease around, too. If anything, he became more promiscuous than before. If he could have, he would probably have put the virus in the water supply."

"Let everyone get it."

"I think he believed—how shall I say it—everyone already had it. He was just making it visible. AIDS was already there, everywhere, in the polluted air, in the devastated earth, in the streets, the schools, the churches—well, everywhere. He became a symbol of the corruption he saw all around him."

The marathoners passed again, this time with one man in the lead, two others half a block behind, and then the pack, running determinedly together. There was no sign of the two fat men. The leader's face was shining, and not just with sweat. He was triumphant, and knew it. I watched him circle the Plaza Vasco de Quiroga. As he passed the far corner he lifted a clenched fist. Above him were black clouds, and the first hints of rain.

"Well," she said at last, "I shall leave Garred in his grave. But I shant forgive him."

"No," I said. "I dont suppose that would be possible."

We sipped at our coffee. After a while I saw one of the fat marathoners. He was walking, almost stumbling, his face purple. He went to a bench and sat down. He sagged there, defeated. There was a red bandana around his forehead. It was clearly foolish for him to have attempted such a run. An official, perhaps concerned, drifted towards him. Then it began to rain, and the wind blew darkly through the trees.

5

Much of this novel was written in Mexican cafes. I remember with fondness the Cafe del Olmo in Morelia, with its sombre lighting, and the Cafe La Flor in Xalapa, where they roasted their own coffee beans. There were sidewalk cafes, too, in Merida and Uruapan and Guanajuato, and other towns. Many of these have unfortunately become expensive and are thus frequented mostly by tourists, who seem a bit dazed by Mexican street life, and local businessmen who resentfully ignore the tourists. Nevertheless I found some cafes that were pleasant, mostly the older ones, not yet spruced up to attract big spending foreigners. I liked the arched portales looking out over the streets, and the old men playing guitars for a few pesos. I liked watching the dark-eyed girls strut by on their high heels, the men gesturing constantly with their hands, the small boys drifting from table to table, selling chiclets, the traffic cops bargaining with motorists who were illegally parked. But my favorite cafe was not open to the street at all. It was the Cafe Excelsior in Aguascalientes. The front part was a bookstore. People gathered at the tables in back, talking and gesticulating, sometimes with passion. It was possible in the Excelsior to play chess, to argue politics, to compare Jorge Luis Borges to Octavio Paz, to contrast Velasquez to Goya. Odd things could happen there. A lady once sat at my table and gave me a rose. She stared for a long time into my eyes. "My mother killed her five children," she finally said. "I'm sorry to hear that," I responded politely, and returned to my book and coffee. When I left an hour later she was still there, still staring. Rosa Maria, at the counter, shrugged her shoulders. Once I saw a chess player get angry and knock over the board, not because he wasnt winning—he was—but because his opponent was taking too much time in losing. With Susan, who had married into a wealthy Mexican family, I discussed photography and the failings of modern psychology; and with Dan, a missionary, I argued the lineage of Arianism and the Christian ideals of Nikos Kazantzakis. Elida and I discussed Mexican politics and American culture, and Jose and I the difficulty of a life devoted to art. Yolanda and Norma, like two flowers, blossomed at my table, admired by all. All this was possible in the Excelsior, and other Mexican cafes. And none of it, alas, would be possible—

"—in American cafes."

"That's right."

"What do they talk about in America?"

"What kind of car to buy, what was on TV last night—the prices of things, like cigarettes—which athletic shoe is the one to get this season—"

"And this is where you want to take me?"

"Well, just for a while. You should see it."

"I hardly ever wear athletic shoes."

"I noticed."

She turned her foot so we could both see her instep, which was arched in her red, high-heeled shoe. We had gone back to the hotel and changed—myself into faded jeans and a gray jacket over a white shirt, she into a tight black skirt and her heels. When the rain let up we strolled to the Fuente de Sodas Tim's, near El Santuario. We were sipping again at coffees, for her a Capuchino, for me a Cafe Americano, black and rich. On the street outside, people had already gathered. Tables were set out. At the iron gates of the church stood a white-robed priest surrounded by his faithful. All of us awaited the parade, which would end here. It was darkening outside, and yellow lights had begun to glow in the shops. The street was emptied of cars. There were only people murmuring, and the dark clouds tumbling overhead.

While we waited I told her more about Virginia White. Originally I had seen her crawling out from the ruins of the cross-shaped building. The earth was glazed under the brilliant sun. Flies buzzed around bodies, half in and half out of the rubble. In the red garden a broken helicopter smouldered. There was no sign of Garred, no sign of Osgood. Virginia herself was bloodied, bruised. All she wore was her brassiere, its one cup still intact, thanks, of course, to the supply in the wardrobe woman's closet. It was rather interesting, watching one breast bound, one breast unbound; one contained, one wobbling. But her face was awful: left side swollen, black, still bleeding, the eye closed, teeth missing. Her long blonde hair fell everywhere, like dirty straw tossed in the wind. She crawled down from the rubble in a series of close-ups and medium shots, and then stood in the open space, near a crater, while the camera backed away and rose into the sky, thus emphasizing her isolation. Finally she moved off, a tiny, solitary figure, down the dirt road towards the town. Within the town were only more bodies—soldiers sprawling from windows, lying amongst shell casings in doorways—but at the train station was a great mob of people, coppery-eyed natives, women crying, children wailing, men hurrying to and fro. At last a train came. Everyone pushed to get on board, including Virginia White: white flesh pressed amid all that copper. It was a struggle for her. She cried in pain. But at last she got in, just as the train started to move and people fell back to the tracks. She was shunted up against the door at one end, squeezed there, scarcely able to breathe. For a while the camera just stared at her, moved in close to her panicky face.

Then she turned and looked through the window. There was another carriage behind the one she was in. Three men were there. They wore gray slacks and white shirts. They looked like oil company executives. All were Europeans with short, well-brushed hair. They were studying sheaves of paper, which they passed back and forth. Virginia banged on her window. She pressed her face against the glass. She kicked at the door. At last one of the men looked up. There was no expression discernible on his face. He walked down the corridor, past the leather seats, to the door of his carriage. His face was thus no more than thirty-six inches from hers. It remained expressionless. It was partially obscured by sunlight glancing off the glass. Then he reached up and pulled down a shade. Virginia White slid slowly to the floor.

6

It was not quite dark outside. The crowd had grown, but they were quiet. We could hear fireworks exploding in the distance.

"But you chose a different ending?"

"There didnt seem to be a choice. An ending eventually writes itself. One simply has to step back out of its way, and let it proceed—sometimes in directions one doesnt expect. I could not force Virginia White out of the rubble, into that train."

"She balked."

"What she did was just get up, walk off the set, and return to Iowa."

"Dressed, I hope, in more than that torn bra."

"Yes, yes. Her face bandaged, too."

"Did the production company pay her bills? It sounds like she needed extensive care—a doctor, a dentist—"

"And plastic surgery. But no. The company immediately declared bankruptcy, and the principals vanished from sight. Only Garred got anything—he had insisted on half his pay up front. The rest were lucky they survived."

She flew to Iowa. The jet hissed through the sky for hours. She changed planes once, perhaps twice. She was shuttled down one chute, up another. Anonymous hands plucked at her clothes, her breasts, her buttocks. In Iowa she immediately married a cocky, bow-legged man, considerably older than her, who worked in sales. The plastic surgery and dental work they could afford could not entirely restore her face; and scar tissue had built up within her vagina and cervix, making intercourse difficult and pregnancy impossible. At first she tried to resume her previous life. She tried to behave as though everything were normal. But nothing was normal any more. She began to eat. She went on food binges. Sometimes she threw up afterwards, on purpose, but the vomiting made her sick. So she just ate and drank. She grew as bloated as the bodies in the rice paddies. One day she cut off her long blonde hair. After that she would not go out. Her husband had to do all the shopping. He didnt seem to mind at first. He brought home bottles of Jack Daniels and Hiram Walker coffee flavored brandy and all the cakes and pies and ice cream she wanted. He continued to brag at work about his moviestar wife. He would take out photographs and show them to everyone. When people wanted to meet her, he would compare her to Greta Garbo: she just wanted to be left alone. He didnt tell anyone she was fat. Virginia sat all day in front of the television, watching soap operas, old movies, and Phil Donahue. She ate and drank. After a while her husband started to beat her. But it was never very serious. He just slapped her around a little. The bruises hardly showed. He grew a paunch himself and started losing his hair. The day he made vice-president in charge of sales, he came home drunk, found his wife snoring on the floor, and beat her more intensely than he ever had before. The next day, however, he apologized. Sometimes he watched television with her. Her eyes had sunk into her cheeks, and were scarcely visible. She overflowed the chair. Her bed had to be reinforced. She didnt leave the house again until she died a few years later. Doors had to be removed so her corpse could exit. Her husband put a photograph of her on the casket, so everyone could see how beautiful his wife had been. The casket itself was closed. He respected, he said, his wife's wish for privacy. But he continued to take photographs from his wallet to show people, especially when he drank. Some were publicity stills, and quite professionally sexy. He did this even after he remarried. His second wife was thin, pale, lackluster, and spent much of her time sleeping. He had no photographs of her.

7

She was silent. We went out onto the street. After a while she began to talk. While she talked, the night descended. More people pressed around us. Three tourists passed, two girls and a pale boy, speaking German. They were dressed in the ragged remnants of their civilization.

"You are hard on women," she said. "I dont think you can claim innocence in this affair. To some degree you must admit Virginia White is your creation. No, no. Dont interrupt. I know as much about art as you do. I do not deny the independence of your creations, or the people who portray them. But you put her in harm's way. You set everything in motion. If you had selected someone stronger than Virginia White you would have had an entirely different ending—an entirely different story. You knew quite well—from the beginning— that her survival was in doubt. You degraded her. She did not deserve such torment. Bloated, indeed—like a dead body in a rice paddy. I'm surprised you didnt have her intestines spill out. How did you describe it? 'Great looping coils.' This work has become perverse. I wonder if every woman you are associated with is so brutalized. You are deceptive. You talk about masks. Do you ever reveal your true form? If I remove this mask from you, is there another one below it? Do you imagine you are one of those god-impersonators, manipulating everyone around you? What are your plans for me? Is there something you have in mind that you would like to explain to me? Do you have a script for me to read? If you think I am going to slavishly follow your directions you are quite mistaken. I am not a foolish innocent like

Virginia White and the rest of your American friends. You will not catch me unaware. You are a cruel man. Cruel, and perverse."

The rocket man came up the street. He held the rockets between thumb and forefinger and lit them with the glowing tip of a cigarette. The rockets shot up into the air, making sizzling noises, and then exploded. A boy trailed behind, handing him the rockets. The cigarette glowed ochre.

"Look," I said. "Here's the parade."

It was led by a police car and boys carrying a large portrait of the Virgin Mother. Then came taxis—there must have been fifty of them, perhaps every taxi in town—all maroon and white and festooned with ribbons and balloons and crepe. On the hoods rode little girls in frilly white frocks. We were silent, watching them. The crowd pressed us close together. I took her arm, and felt her hip against mine. After the taxis came beribboned buses, belching fumes. The crowd was quite silent: women dressed in their best clothes, men in straw hats and gleaming shoes, children made up like dolls. We could hear music approaching, and at last, following the buses, came groups of men playing accordions and saxophones and bass fiddles and guitars and drums. Interspersed were more portraits of the Virgin, held aloft, her serene, indifferent face high above the crowd. The taxis, buses, and trucks turned left at the corner. But the people all went forward, through the iron gates, into the church courtyard. After the last band the spectators spilled onto the street. People were packed curb to curb, marching to the Parroquia. We let them press past us with difficulty. Anonymous shoulders, breasts, hips pushed against us. We worked our way back to the sidewalk and to a table covered with Coke bottles and bowls and a large pot of pozole steaming over a brazier. We wedged ourselves against the wall. An old man gave us bowls. The pozole was hot and rich. I watched her spoon it into her mouth. I watched her lips part, and her tongue emerge.

A yellow light glowed above her, casting shadows down her face. She turned her eyes to me.

"I said you are cruel," she said.

"I wont argue with you."

"And perverse."

"I acknowledge what you say."

Her lips were painted so they were almost black. She put down her bowl.

"Pay him," she ordered.

I gave the man two thousand pesos.

"Rico," I said.

"Sí, muy rico."

He grinned up at me. His teeth were brown. The woman pulled my arm.

"I want something sweet," she said.

We pushed through the crowd. I put my hands on her hips. My fingers felt around to her belly, where her belly narrowed into her crotch. She stopped at a stall where a woman made pancakes. The old woman smeared cajeta on a pancake and handed it up. I paid, and we moved on. "My fingers are sticky," she said after a moment. She stopped and turned so she faced me. I could see the cajeta, syrupy, on her fingers. She began to lick at her fingers. I watched her for a moment and then took her wrist. I put her fingers into my mouth. Her face was expressionless, but after a moment her lips parted. At the corner the crowd eased. A rain began to fall. I watched the droplets gather in her hair. As we crossed the plaza the yellow lights on their poles made her hair luminesce. When she shook her head, the lights in her hair scattered away. Our faces became damp. Drops of water rolled down my shirt, and down her blouse. At the far corner of the plaza men and women shivered around a stall selling seafood. Their faces turned in our direction. A gas fire hissed. Our feet made little splashes in the water glowing on the street. All the lights—the street lights, the lights in the buildings—reflected up from the puddles beneath us. We were illuminated from above and below. As we hurried forward the lights kept shifting. Sleek sheets of water rippled as we stepped into them. Her hair was wet. Her eyelashes were wet. I saw water at her throat. We went faster.

In our room she stopped and turned. She seemed very tall and dark. I could smell her wet clothes. I pushed her onto the bed. Her black skirt bunched up at her waist. Her white thighs lifted over my shoulders. "No," she said after a moment. "Oh, no," she moaned. "No, not that." Her white body began to buck. Her red shoes kicked in the air. I raised myself over her. Our eyes met. In her eyes I saw horror, and pain, and desperation, and greed. I hovered there, above her, while she stared up at me. Rain spat against a window. Her blouse was torn open. One breast lay exposed. She stared up at me. I hovered there, on my outstretched arms, raised above her.

"My lizard," she said. *"My lizard."*

I plunged into her, into oblivion.

RECENT TITLES FROM FC2

From the District File
A novel by Kenneth Bernard
From the District File depicts a bureaucratic world of supercontrolled
oppressiveness in the not-too-distant future. *Publishers Weekly* calls
Bernard's fiction "a confrontation with the inexpressible...a provocative
comment on the restrictiveness and pretension of our lives."
128 pages, Cloth: $18.95, Paper: $8.95

Double or Nothing
A novel by Raymond Federman
"Invention of this quality ranks the book among the fictional masterpieces
of our age...I have read *Double or Nothing* several times and am not
finished with it yet, for it is filled with the kinds of allusion and complex-
ity that scholars will feast upon for years. Were literature a stock market,
I'd invest in this book"—Richard Kostelanetz
300 pages, Paper: $10.95

F/32
A novel by Eurudice
F/32 is a wild, eccentric, Rabaelaisian romp through most forms of
amorous excess. But, it is also a troubling tale orbiting around a public
sexual assault on the streets of Manhattan. Between the poles of desire
and butchery, the novel and Ela sail, the awed reader going along for one
of the most dazzling rides in recent American fiction.
276 pages, Cloth: $18.95, Paper, $8.95

Trigger Dance
Stories by Diane Glancy
"Diane Glancy writes with poetic knowledge of Native Americans...The
characters of *Trigger Dance* do an intricate dance that forms wonderful new
story patterns. With musical language, Diane Glancy teaches us to hear
ancient American refrains amidst familiar American sounds. A beautiful
book."—Maxine Hong Kingston
137 pages, Cloth: $18.95, Paper: $8.95

Is It Sexual Harassment Yet?
Stories by Cris Mazza
"The stories...continually surprise, delight, disturb, and amuse. Mazza's
'realism' captures the eerie surrealism of violence and repressed sexuality
in her characters' lives."—Larry McCaffery
226 pages, Cloth: $18.95, Paper: 8.95

Napoleon's Mare
A novella by Lou Robinson
Napoleon's Mare, thirteen chapters and a section of prose poems is a diatribe, a discontinuous narrative—as much about writing as about the bewildering process of constructing a self.
177 pages, Cloth: $18.95, Paper: $8.95

Valentino's Hair
A novel by Yvonne Sapia
"Intense and magical, *Valentino's Hair* vividly creates an America intoxicated by love and death. Sapia brilliantly renders the vitality and tensions in the Puerto Rican community in 1920s New York City."—Jerome Stern. Picked as one of the top 25 books for 1991 by Publishers Weekly.
162 pages, Cloth: $18.95, Paper: $8.95

Mermaids for Attila
Stories by Jacques Servin
Mermaids for Attila is a fun, hands-on, toy-like book on the subject of well-orchestrated national behaviors. In it Servin considers the biggest horrors and the weirdest political truths. "At a time when conventional narrative fiction is making an utterly boring comeback, it is a relief to find writers like Jacques Servin who are willing to acknowledge that verbal representation can no longer be regarded as anything more than a point of departure."—Stephen-Paul Martin
128 pages, Cloth: $18.95, Paper: $8.95

Hearsay
A novel by Peter Spielberg
Hearsay is a darkly comic account of the misadventures of one Lemuel Grosz from youthbed to deathbed. In its blending of reality and irreality, *Hearsay* present a life the way we winess the life of another: from a certain distance, catching a glimpse here, a revelation there.
275 pages, Cloth: $18.95, Paper: $8.95

Close Your Eyes and Think of Dublin: Portrait of a Girl
A novel by Kathryn Thompson
A brilliant Joycean hallucination of a book in which the richness of Leopold Bloom's inner life is found in a young American girl experiencing most of the things that vexed James Joyce: sex, church, and oppression.
197 pages, Cloth: $18.95, Paper: $8.95

Books may be ordered through the Talman Company, 150 Fifth Avenue, New York, NY 10011.

For a catalog listing all books published by Fiction Collective, write to Fiction Collective Two, Department of English, Illinois State University, Normal, IL 61761-6901.